ACTS of
COURAGE

Laura Secord and the War of 1812

A Commemorative Edition Published
for the Bicentennial Anniversary
of the War of 1812

ACTS of
COURAGE

Laura Secord and the War of 1812

CONNIE BRUMMEL CROOK

Text copyright © 2012 Connie Brummel Crook
This edition copyright © 2012 Pajama Press Inc.
This is a first edition.
10 9 8 7 6 5 4 3 2 1

www.pajamapress.ca   info@pajamapress.ca

The publisher gratefully acknowledges the support of the Canada Council for the Arts and the Ontario Arts Council for its publishing program. We acknowledge the financial support of the Government of Canada through the Book Publishing Industry Development Program (BPIDP) for our publishing activities.

Canada Council   Conseil des Arts   ONTARIO ARTS COUNCIL
for the Arts   du Canada   CONSEIL DES ARTS DE L'ONTARIO

Library and Archives Canada Cataloguing in Publication

Crook, Connie Brummel

    Acts of courage : Laura Secord and the War of 1812 / Connie Brumel Crook.

ISBN 978-0-9869495-7-9

    1. Secord, Laura, 1775-1868--Juvenile fiction. 2. Canada--

History--War of 1812--Juvenile fiction. I. Title.

PS8555.R6113A77 2012   jC813'.54   C2011-908603-4

U.S. Publisher Cataloging-in-Publication Data (U.S.)

Brummel Crook, Connie
    Acts of courage: Laura Secord and the War of 1812 / Connie Brummel Crook.
[ ] p. : maps ; cm.
From title page: a commemorative edition published for the bicentennial anniversary
of the War of 1812.
Summary: The story of Laura Ingersoll Secord, from her early days in Massachusetts and her family's immigration to Upper Canada to her part in the War of 1812, when she rescued her injured husband on the field of battle and undertook a dangerous twenty mile trek to warn the British commander of an impending American attack on the British outpost at Beaver Dams.
ISBN-13: 978-0-9869495-7-9 (pbk.)
1. Secord, Laura Ingersoll – Juvenile fiction. 2. Beaver Dams, Battle of, Beaver Dams, Ont., 1813 – Juvenile fiction. 3. United States—History — War of 1812 — Campaigns –Juvenile fiction.
[Fic] dc23   PZ7.B786ac 2012

Book and cover design–Rebecca Buchanan
Cover Illustrations–Brian Deines

Manufactured by Webcom. Printed in Canada.

MIX
Paper from
responsible sources
FSC® C004071
www.fsc.org

Pajama Press Inc.
469 Richmond St E, Toronto Ontario, Canada
www.pajamapress.ca

To my dear father, Elick T. Brummel (1907-1992),
who loved to read and retell tales of our own
Canadian past, including this one;
and to my devoted mother, Pearl Carr Brummel (1911-2006),
who toiled willingly for her family,
even as Laura Secord did.

ACKNOWLEDGEMENTS

I would like to thank the Niagara Falls Public Library for allowing me to read their files on Laura Secord; the reference department of Peterborough Public Library for obtaining books and photocopied materials through the inter-library loan program; and the reference department of Trent University Bata library for helping find historical background material.

Thanks also to Nancy Watt, a teacher at Huron Heights High School, Newmarket, and director of Period Fashion Seminars, whom I consulted about clothing.

Thanks to Peter Johnson of Frankford, Ontario, a retired teacher of Secondary School Art in Scarborough, Ontario, for his detailed maps tracing the Ingersolls' journey to Upper Canada and also showing the route of Laura's famous walk.

A very special thanks to Gavin K. Watt of King City, Ontario, Past President and Founder of the Museum of Applied Military History, military consultant for the film *Divided Loyalties* and recipient of the Toronto Historical Board's Commendation for "extraordinary effort in perpetuating Canada's Military Heritage," for answering my many questions about the military, firearms, equipment, and grooming.

Thanks also to my husband Albert who accompanied me to the Laura Secord sites and helped me to trace the route of her famous walk.

Thanks to Ann and Grenfell Featherstone for their careful editing, and to Gail Winskill, Publisher of Pajama Press, for her support and encouragement.

CONTENTS

❧

THE INGERSOLLS' JOURNEY
TO UPPER CANADA

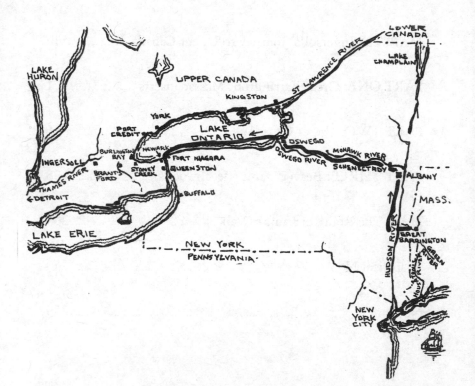

Part One
Great Barrington, Massachusetts

ONE

The door burst open and a gust of raw wind blew across the classroom. The town watchman, his face red from the cold, strode over to the teacher, Mr. Salisbury. His serious expression told Laura that the watchman had brought bad news.

Mr. Salisbury straightened his glasses and cleared his throat. "All after-school lessons and practices are cancelled," he announced. "Go straight home. Do not linger along the roadside and do not take any shortcuts across fields."

"Why?" asked Thomas Mayo. He didn't look worried. In fact, he had a smug look on his face. Laura Ingersoll wondered if the rumours were true—that Thomas secretly belonged to the rebels. She knew many farmers supported them.

"Because the agitators are on the prowl again," the schoolmaster explained. "They have never hurt children, but it would be best to avoid them. Keep to the main roads. Now, hurry and go."

As she raced down the front steps of the school, Laura shivered inside her red wool cloak and pulled the hood tightly over her head. She was used to seeing soldiers and bands of men passing along this way to Great Barrington. The town was close to the main boundary between Massachusetts and New York, and it had been a centre of traffic during the Revolutionary War that had ended four years before in 1783.

The sun was shining so brightly in the southwestern sky that Laura had to squint her eyes. It was going to be a bitter February evening, so she hurried along the road with the hard snow crunching under her feet. Her family lived just south of the town, almost a mile away. She passed sleighs with waiting parents—but not hers. She knew no one would be waiting for her. Of course, it couldn't be helped, for her mother had died four years before, and her new stepmother, Mercy, was always sick. Her father was never home.

As she turned off the front street of Great Barrington and onto the main highway leading south out of town, Laura heard the crunch of footsteps just behind.

"Wait up, Laura," shouted Elizabeth Bachus. Elizabeth was the new girl at school. She had arrived from New York just after Christmas and lived with her mother on her grandparents' estate, just a mile beyond Laura's house.

Elizabeth was shivering, and her face was beet red from the raw wind.

"This is a dreadful place to live," said Elizabeth with a frown. "I wish Mother would take us right back to New York City."

Laura had heard the rumour that Elizabeth's grandfather, Judge Whiting, was tired of paying his daughter's expenses in New York City.

"My grandparents persuaded Mother to come home, since Grandma took sick."

"My stepmother is sick a lot, too."

"You mean you don't have a real mother?" said Elizabeth.

"Of course I have a real mother...but she's dead."

"I can't remember much about my father. Most of the time, he was away in the army. So I don't miss him."

"My father's always away," said Laura.

"My grandpa was never away much when *he* was judge of Great Barrington...before he retired."

"My father's more than just judge of Great Barrington. He's also captain of the local militia."

"So I suppose he's out chasing rebels today. That's too bad."

Laura wasn't even sure that she was proud of her father for helping to put down the uprising. After all, many of the farmers were rebelling because they couldn't pay their taxes. Many had their farms taken away, and some had even been sent to prison for debts.

"Do you think there'll be a real battle? My mother says—"

Elizabeth's words were cut short by the sound of tramping feet and loud laughter just up ahead.

"It's them! It must be," gasped Elizabeth.

Three figures in tattered homespun breeches and woollen coats walked toward them on the opposite side of the road. The first two were middle-aged farmers with unshaven faces and straggly hair. Laura wouldn't have wanted to meet them alone!

Elizabeth grabbed Laura's arm. They gripped hands tightly and kept to the outer edge of their own side of the road as they plodded toward the strangers. There was no escape across the snow-filled fields, and if they turned and ran toward town, the men would soon catch them. Elizabeth stopped suddenly, but Laura pulled her ahead, for she knew it was better to keep going. Even now they were in sight of Laura's home across the fields.

"Well, if it isn't Little Red Riding Hood." One of the men pointed at Laura's red cloak and laughed through his nose.

"Going to Grandma's house?" the man jeered. He stepped into the middle of the road, closer to the trembling girls.

Laura noticed a boy behind them. His red hair blew wildly in the wind, and his tattered doeskin coat hung loosely from his shoulders. He looked no older than the boys in her class. Laura could hardly believe it. Her father hadn't told her there would be boys that young in this rebellion. But she did remember him saying that the militia would stop the rebels before they reached Great Barrington. So what were they doing here?

"What're you afraid of?" the nearest man sneered at Elizabeth, whose hands were shaking hard now. "The big bad wolf?"

Laura yanked Elizabeth by the hand and started to run from the men.

Her heart thumped heavily with the strain of pulling Elizabeth, and she was soon winded. But when she looked over her shoulder, she saw only the men's backs. They were heading on toward the town. She heard a ripple of laughter coming from their direction.

"They've gone on," she said bravely, now that the crisis had passed.

"Are you sure?" Elizabeth, too, was gasping for breath. "C'mon, in case they change their minds." She let go of Laura's hand and stumbled on ahead.

Laura turned back for one more look. The men were just two dark figures by now, but the boy was still easy to see. He was walking some distance behind the others. She couldn't help admiring the defiant way he marched down the road. Then, unexpectedly, he spun around and seemed to stare at Laura before he turned back and sauntered on behind the men.

"Why are you staring at those rascals?" Elizabeth shouted. Laura turned and started walking toward home again. "I just can't understand why you'd stop to look at that grubby bunch. It's a good job you had me along to drag you away."

"*I'm* the one who dragged *you* away! I only stopped after we were past them."

"Really. So why did you take the time to stare at that stupid boy?"

"I was just looking at…" Laura couldn't think of any reason. She clenched her mittened hands tightly together underneath her cloak and, taking long strides, pushed ahead. Elizabeth followed a few steps behind.

They had not walked much farther when sleigh bells rang out just ahead of them. "It's Grandpa!" Elizabeth ran toward the sleigh.

Judge Whiting made a sharp turn in his covered cutter and drew up beside the girls. "Hop in," he said. "You, too, Laura Ingersoll. I'm sorry to be late. It looks as if you didn't have games after school today."

"I don't need a ride, thank you," Laura said. "I'm almost home. I'll walk."

"Young lady, you get in the sleigh this minute. I'm taking you right to your door." Laura could see there was no point in arguing. She stepped up onto the iron footstep on the side of the cutter and sat beside Elizabeth, who had wrapped herself up in the bearskin lap rug. She unfolded a side of the rug and threw it across Laura's lap.

"Now, girls," said the judge, "next time school gets out early, you wait till I get there. You can't be too careful these days. And, Laura, I know your father is away on business, but you should have waited until one of his servants came for you."

"Bett and Sam are too busy. My stepmother had another bad spell, and Bett's afraid it's pneumonia. Mira's still at home, you know. She's only six, and Bett has to take care of her, too."

"I see." The judge took out of his handkerchief and blew his nose. "Well, we'll stop for you tomorrow morning. Be ready at eight. I always like Elizabeth to be on time."

They rode on in silence, right to the long lane leading to Laura's home. Judge Whiting turned the cutter between the cedar and red pine that stood on either side of the lane to the house. Through the trees, Laura could see part of the thirty acres of land that her father owned. It was enough to raise a few young cattle and grow a vegetable garden to supply most of the family food.

As they came up to the house, Laura saw Sam, their black slave, heading across the yard toward the barn to do the chores.

"Whoa!" The judge drew his horses to a halt in front of the white frame house.

Laura jumped down into the deep snow beside the cutter before it came to a full stop.

"Thank you, sir," she shouted as she stepped onto the path leading to the front of the house.

She ran up to the verandah and hurried along it to the side kitchen door. She was shivering from the cold and snow. Inside the kitchen, her cheeks tingled in the warmth from the fire crackling in the hearth.

"Where's Bett?" Laura asked her sister, Mira, who ran up and put her arms around Laura's snowy cloak.

"Putting a mustard plaster on Mama—ooh, you're all wet—she coughs all the time now."

"Has Father come home?"

"No. Want to see my new doll? Sam made it." Mira held up a small wooden doll with an acorn head.

"That's nice," said Laura without looking at the doll. She walked into the front hall and hung her red cloak on its hook. She could hear her stepmother's sharp coughing from the room at the top of the stairs.

Back in the kitchen, Laura sat down beside Mira on the horsehair couch in front of the fireplace. As Mira snuggled up to her, Laura gazed out the window. Through the swirling snow, she could see three dark figures making their way alongside of the barn. Laura's heart beat faster as she realized they were the same men she and Elizabeth had met on the way home from school. And the red-headed boy was there, too, straggling along behind.

Laura rushed to the door and flung it open, but they had vanished. All she could hear was the howling of the wind as it whipped across the bare verandah.

TWO

A shaft of light beaming through the iced-up windows wakened Laura. The rest of the family was already downstairs eating breakfast. She could hear spoons scraping against the wooden porridge bowls, and Mira whining about something to Bett. Laura pulled the quilt over her head to muffle the sounds and keep out the cold. If she stayed in bed for just a little longer, she might be able to walk to school by herself. There was no point in getting out from under the quilts before she had to.

She had not lain there long before she heard the back kitchen door slam shut and Bett saying, "No, don't wait, Elizabeth. Laura isn't up yet. So she'll just have to walk. Thank your grandpa for callin', though." Then, after the front door closed, she heard Bett say, "Now where's that Laura? It isn't like her to lie in bed after me callin' her twice."

Laura was out of bed in a bound. It might be cold out

there, but it would be worse to get a scolding from Bett. She had a way of saying things that were true, but you didn't want to hear. In minutes, Laura was almost dressed and downstairs. She only had to lace up the front of her gown and put her boots on.

"Why, there you are! Whatever came over to you to lie in bed so long?" Bett opened her eyes wide at Laura and raised one eyebrow.

"Well...," Laura began.

"Oh, never mind now. I see you're all ready and rarin' to go, so eat your porridge quick and get out that door." Laura did up her boots and gown as quickly as she could and gulped down her breakfast. Then she grabbed her wool cloak off the peg in the hallway and raced out the back. Bett's words followed her. "Hurry on to school, now. Those agitators are still out on the roads, and the longer you linger the more's the chance you'll be in their way. Lord help us. This is no place for children to grow up in."

It was a snowy day. The wind was blowing but, between gusts, the sun shone down in blinding rays. She rounded the side of the house and went down the front lane. She had just turned to the left onto the highway that led to Great Barrington when she heard men's voices and laughter carried on the wind from the cedar woods to the east of the highway. She kept walking along the road, but she looked in the direction of the sounds and thought she saw glinting steel between the cedar branches about one hundred feet away. She should head back home. But curiosity got the better of her, and she stepped off the left side of the road, opposite the sound, and hid behind a clump of wild raspberry bushes.

Through the swirling snow, she saw a crowd of nearly a hundred men. They emerged from the woods and strode toward the highway. Most were well armed with rifles and muskets, and some carried other supplies. A few, who appeared to be no older than Thomas and Levi Mayo, straggled along farther back. Some were regular soldiers, but many wore tattered farmers' clothes that still gave off the sharp smell of pig manure.

The band of men turned down the highway toward town and passed right by her. Just as Laura thought that she should risk making a run for it back home, she heard more heavy tramping and saw the next group coming toward her. They were prodding a prisoner along the way—ahead of them. With a start, Laura realized it was Solomon Gleazen, the schoolmaster from the nearby town of Stockbridge. He looked straight ahead, the way he had when he'd led their spelling bee, but he walked with a noticeable limp and was shivering in his light woollen waistcoat. The man just behind him was wearing a tailored coat much like the one Mr. Gleazen had worn the week before.

Laura shivered. She had to get moving or she would freeze. As the men disappeared from view in the distance, she slowly stepped back onto the road. There was no question of going to school now. She would head for home.

"Where ya goin', Miss?" said a voice with a strong Irish accent. She turned and almost bumped into the boy she had seen the day before. He was sullen-looking now, and she noticed again the red hair and ragged doeskin coat. He must have been standing right behind her as she watched the men pass by.

"None of your business." Laura swerved around him and fell headlong to the ground. She had tripped over the boy's extended boot. Gritty snow bit into her face as she sprawled on the side of the road.

"Look, you can't go back to warn nobody 'bout us. The men up ahead has got business to take care of, an' they don't need the militia called out because of some gabbin' little girl."

The boy reached out his hand to help Laura up and, still short of breath from having her wind knocked out by the fall, she did not resist. Then, unexpectedly, he pulled her over to a clump of young cedar trees farther back in the woods and yanked her down beside him. In a gentler voice, he said, "We'll just stay here till they've had time to do their job. Then you can go on back wherever it was you was goin'. I'm not gonna harm you none, Miss."

Red-faced and angry, Laura gasped, "Well, that's a fine way to show it, knocking me over like that and then dragging me over here."

"Sorry 'bout that, but I had to stop you fast."

Laura studied him intently as they huddled behind the cedars. The boy's fiery red hair blew around his freckled face. His worn twill breeches were made of farmer's homespun, and one sleeve of his doeskin coat was torn and hung loosely from the shoulder. He was shivering. When he noticed Laura staring at him, he pulled the pieces of his sleeve together.

"Where are you from, anyway?" Laura asked in a whisper.

He stared straight into the trees.

"What are all those men doing in our town?" she asked.

He pushed down a cedar bough and peered out toward the road.

Laura became braver and raised her voice. "How long do you think you can keep me here? I'm not far from home, you know."

He was a little bigger than she was, but she bet he wasn't any older, probably around twelve, too.

Finally, he turned to her and mumbled, "Not long." He stared at her for a minute. "Where was you goin', anyway, by yourself this mornin'?"

"To school. Where else?"

"Not very many girls go to school."

"Well, I do. My father's the judge in this town. He wants his daughter to go to school."

"Really! Is he down at the court house now?"

"No, he's..." She stopped abruptly.

"It don't matter none if you don't tell me. We'll all be goin' soon. We don't mean no harm to nobody in Great Barrington, anyway."

"Then why'd you have the Stockbridge schoolmaster tied up?"

"I don't rightly know. I was here ahead, as a scout, you might say. They just picked him up this morning along the way, I guess."

"I know he's the schoolmaster over at Stockbridge. His students visited our school for a spelling bee last week."

"Spelling bees. Boy, am I glad I don't have to be bothered with that kind of stuff and nonsense."

"What a stupid thing to say! They're fun, especially when you win. You're just jealous 'cause all you do is follow soldiers around the countryside in the freezing snow all day."

"I don't put much store by book learnin'. You think learnin' ABC's is going to put food in the bellies of the starvin' farmers? It didn't help back home in Ireland, and it won't help here. Everywhere I go, the farmers have problems. My father shipped me off from Ireland because his farm was too small for my three brothers and three sisters. He could barely grow enough food for the lot of us. 'Go to America,' he says. 'Uncle Gerald's got no sons to help him to work that farm. Four times as big as ours, it is. And when he's gone, it'll be yours.' So I came. Then, once I got out here to my uncle's farm—what happens? He can't pay the taxes because he can't sell the crop. There was no one with the money to buy it. That's the whole problem. People don't need more schoolin'. They need more money. They need to stop those taxes."

"Well, if the farmers were more educated, maybe they'd manage their farms better. And the government can't help the taxes. They're just as poor as anyone else; my father says a war is very expensive, and so is starting up a new country. And we're paying for both right now. It won't last forever."

"Forever! Even a year is goin' to be too late, Miss. Don't you know nothing? There's farmers starving and going to jail because they can't pay their debts. And there's people like..." The boy looked down to the ground and wiped his face with his sleeve. "There's people like my uncle," he continued, "farm just taken away like that. It wasn't his fault he couldn't pay the debts. And Aunt Mary couldn't take it. She took a fit— never spoke another word after that and dropped dead four days later. Me and Uncle Gerald's alone now, and he's taken to drink."

"Well, why aren't you helping him look for a job or something instead of hanging around with these ruffians? He must be wondering where you are."

"Well, you must be a fine lady with a rich dad to be so ignorant. And what would you say if I were to tell you that my uncle just happened to be one of those ruffians, and we joined up 'cause it was all that was left for us?" The boy's grey-green eyes turned dark. "There's no work for no one out there. So there's nothing left to do but fight. Safety in numbers, you know. At least I get to eat every now and then—instead of not at all."

"Every now and then! You should have regular meals."

"How? Are you going to feed me?"

"Well, yes, in fact, I will," Laura blurted out suddenly, feeling more compassion than fear. The boy's face was stark white behind the freckles, and his hands hung bare and gaunt, poking out of the too-short arms of his doeskin coat.

"You? Feed me breakfast? And how are you going to do that?"

"Well," said Laura, "you're going to follow me down the road a piece to that house at the end of the long lane—see the one with the verandah at the side?" She pulled back some cedar branches so he could see her house. "It's quite safe. There's no one around."

The boy hesitated for a moment, and his eyes softened a bit, but then he seemed to come back to himself. "I won't be awantin' anything from you, Miss. More than likely, you'd be leading me straight into a trap. Besides, I have to stay here. The others are depending on me. And they're getting victuals, anyway."

The boy's speech was interrupted by a commotion from the road. "Move along there," yelled a man. Then they heard the heavy steps of many men coming back along the highway from town. Laura and the boy peered out between the boughs.

One man was prodding another in front of him. "Step up, boy."

Laughter drowned out the rest of the man's words. "What a catch! Two cellars full of food and wine!" More loud laughing followed, and then they heard the tramping of a great mob of men heading toward them.

"Stay still," the boy whispered roughly. "I'll not give you away." Then, almost childishly, he added, "Promise me you'll not tell on us when we're gone."

"I promise," Laura repeated shakily. She certainly didn't want to get in the way of that gang.

Some of the men were drinking wine straight from the jugs as they marched along. All of them were dressed in homespun shirts and breeches—which gave little protection against the intense cold of wind and snow. Only a few wore warm wool coats, and even those were full of holes.

Then Laura noticed a man she knew. It was Nathaniel Sheffield, the man who had been caught stealing at the general store in the centre of town.

"They've freed the prisoners!" Laura whispered hoarsely.

"Not so loud. Are you daft? If they see you, they'll more than likely take you hostage, especially a judge's daughter."

"He's not a judge today," Laura said, wondering why the boy wasn't hauling her onto the road and giving her over himself. "My father's—" Laura stopped herself just before giving away the fact that her father was also a captain, who had left very early yesterday morning to lead troops against rebel farmers just like these.

The men finally passed. The boy had not moved toward them, and Laura was thankful.

"I have to go now," he said gruffly. "Remember your promise."

"I will." Laura watched him start to wade through the snow, heading down the highway in the same direction as the men. "Be careful," she called out softly, surprised to hear herself say the words.

The boy turned and gave her a brief, friendly smile. Then he said sharply, "Better to die by the sword than the halter."

Those were not the boy's words—they were the slogan of Shay's men. Laura knew then. It was against these rebels that her father would lead his troops today.

THREE

Laura arrived late at school, only to discover that classes had been cancelled for the rest of the week. She was relieved that school had been closed.

That afternoon, Judge Whiting came by and told Bett that Elizabeth and her mother were planning to go back to New York City for two weeks, to get away from the dangerous happenings around the countryside.

"Land sake's, child, what you lookin' out the window so much fer to see?" asked Bett, as she folded the fresh laundry. Her husband, Sam, looked over Laura's shoulder to the front window.

"Are you quite deaf already, Laura?" Bett sounded impatient.

"No…I'm sorry. I was just thinking."

"I asked you, what are you lookin' at, out that window?"

"Oh, I'm looking for those men I saw this morning."

"They're long gone now. It's not likely they'll be returnin' this way. Too many furious folks 'round Great Barrington. Folks don't take kindly to havin' a bunch of clumsy fellows stompin' through their homes, takin' their victuals and wine."

"They didn't come to our house."

"No, and I don't rightly know why. Our house was the first they come by. Must be the good Lord protectin' us."

"I guess they were anxious to reach the jail before they stopped anywhere," Sam interrupted his wife. "I heard they let out all the prisoners. Some of 'em just ran loose, but most of 'em joined the rebels and marched on."

"Did they break into many houses after that?" Laura asked.

"Yes, I heard tell they did, but no one was hurt. It's hard to blame a man fer stealin' food when his belly's empty."

"Sam! Watch your tongue! Laura, you can help your sister get ready fer bed now. After that, you'd best go yourself."

Laura took one last look out the west window, but she could hardly see a thing. Night had rolled in over the fields as she had been talking to Bett and Sam. She took Mira by the hand and led her up the front stairs. The little girl stared up at her sister with her huge brown eyes and said, "Tell me the story about—"

"Sh-sh, Mira, we're going past Mother Mercy's room," said Laura. She never liked going past her stepmother's room these days. There was always a painful sound of coughing or such a dark silence. The girls passed on tiptoe and turned into their bedroom two doors down the hall. A beam of moonlight stretched over the two four-poster beds by the far wall and landed just short of the cherry-and-maple-wood dresser near the door. Laura remembered a night long ago when the moon had shone in just like this and her mother—her real one—had put her to bed, the way she was putting Mira to bed now.

Mother Mercy started coughing, and Laura tried to drown out the noise by singing to Mira. It was then that Laura heard the low vibrating sound of marching feet. She tucked Mira in, rushed over to the window, and pulled back the heavy linen curtains.

There was just enough moonlight to see soldiers coming along the highway, prodding a crowd of captives ahead of them—maybe fifty altogether. Some of the prisoners were men from the morning's mob. At least three lifeless bodies were draped over the horses. Laura gasped. A small boy no taller than Laura herself stumbled along between two soldiers. It had to be the starving boy she'd met that morning.

Laura went back to Mira and whispered, "I'll be back soon," but the little girl was already asleep.

Laura crept out into the hallway, tiptoed down the front stairs, and took her red cloak off the hook in the downstairs hall. Bett and Sam were arguing about the day's events, so Laura was able to slip out the front without being noticed. In the cold, still air of the night, she felt suddenly frightened and alone, but she forced herself to walk down the lane to the highway, keeping well behind the soldiers marching toward town. When they stopped, she stepped in behind the undergrowth of young cedar bushes that grew thick along their lane.

"That boy's bound to be nearby. We'll catch him later," she could hear one soldier saying. "He can't go far. Besides, we better put these fellows safely away first."

"Yeah," another soldier said. "We got to attend to the dead. Poor Solomon. It wasn't his battle. I wonder why they forced him along."

"As a hostage, I suppose. The miserable pigs! You can never tell what a mob will do. But this'll be the end of Daniel Shay and his motley rebels, I warrant. There'll be many a hanging after this day."

"They say our judge will soon be a major, instead of a captain."

"What's that got to do with anything?"

"Didn't you see how he led the defence? He's bound to be promoted for that."

"He isn't much like Judge Whiting, is he?"

"Oh?"

"Judge Whiting takes the side of the farmers in the rebellion. He says he can't blame them none. Times are rough for these guys."

"Still, there must be a better way—guess that kid's gone.

We can pick him up later."

Laura stood in shocked silence. Those men were talking about her father; she was sure they were. And about Elizabeth's grandfather, too. But beyond that, she didn't know what to think. Her relief at knowing he was still alive was soon replaced with anger at his so-called success. Who did he think he was, leading soldiers against these poor people and pummeling them to death? Couldn't he just frighten them into running back to their farms?

Suddenly, a firm hand clamped over Laura's mouth. A cold fear gripped her as she tried to twist herself away.

"It's me, miss. Don't yell, an' I'll let go."

Laura nodded. The hand gradually moved away from her mouth. She tasted dirt on her lips. She turned around gingerly, wiping her mouth with the back of her hand.

She was not surprised to see that it was the boy she had met in the morning. He looked tired but meaner. Laura was beginning to wish she'd never come out, but she didn't want to let on she was scared.

"What are you going to do now?" she said roughly.

"Don't know. Guess I'll head back through Stockbridge and to the hills. Lots of places to hide in them hills." At these words, the boy looked so defeated that Laura lost all her fear. His eyes were sunken, and his face was cold and red.

"There's a storm starting," she said.

"Maybe so, but I can't stay here. They'll soon be searchin' everywhere for the strays." He looked at the snowflakes that were beginning to fall.

"They won't search our house because my father's a judge."

He stared back at her in disbelief before saying in a squeaky voice, "What 'bout the judge, hisself?"

"He's away," she tried to reassure the boy. Now he was the one who was scared.

"Still, I don't like it." His tone was firmer now.

"I could take you to our neighbours. They're out in the country a bit."

"How do I know it's not a trap?"

"You don't. Look, you can strike out in the storm if you wish, and they'll soon be combing the countryside for you. If you don't collapse in the storm or get lost, the soldiers will pick you up for sure."

He glanced down the road where the soldiers had gone. Then, as he turned to leave, he looked at Laura and hesitated. He stood still for a minute and then, reluctantly, slumped down onto a fallen limb. He sat there, staring ahead as the snow began to fall thick on the ground.

"Well, maybe it's not such a bad idea," he mumbled.

Laura led the ragged boy through the snow, across the field in the direction of Thomas and Levi's house, where Laura knew they'd find a place for the boy to hide. As they walked past Laura's home, the wind picked up from the north and cut them right to the bone with cold.

"It's not far," she said, although the farm was almost a mile away. Then, without warning, the boy stumbled and fell face first into the deep snow. Laura held out her mittened hand to help him, but he brushed the snow from his face and struggled to his feet by himself.

A few minutes later, he stumbled again and this time let Laura help. Her hand in his, Laura pulled him along, and by the time they staggered into the Mayos' yard, the boy collapsed into a snowbank at the foot of their lane. Laura left him half-conscious while she walked on up the lane to the house and knocked on the back kitchen door.

A chair scraped on the rough floorboards, footsteps came toward her, and the door creaked open. Thomas poked his nose out. "Laura Ingersoll! Whatever are you doing here at this hour? Hey, Levi, it's little Laura! Maybe she's brought over another stray."

They always teased her about that sick kitten she'd brought them, and then found it was a baby raccoon. But she ignored the remark and beckoned Thomas out onto the stone stoop. "I've brought a farm lad who needs help." She knew the Mayo family were sympathetic toward the rebels. In fact, she'd even heard Sam say that the boys might have been involved in Shay's uprising.

Thomas stopped himself in the middle of a snicker. "I'll get Levi, and we'll be right out." He left the door ajar as he stepped back inside.

Still struggling to get into their wool coats, the Mayo brothers hurried out onto the back stoop and followed Laura to where the boy was lying in a crumpled heap in the snow. They rolled him over onto his back and felt for his pulse. He made only a few groaning sounds.

"This boy's suffering from frostbite and exposure. We'll have to get him warm," Thomas said.

"We don't dare take him into the barn or even the house," Levi explained to her. "Lincoln's calling in more militia. It seems a number escaped today, and they'll be scouring the countryside. The word is they're going to make examples of all these fellows, and squash the rebellion once and for all."

"I have it!" said Thomas. "We'll take him to the potato hole. Levi, you go back and get a pot of live coals. That'll give us enough heat. I'll get a straw pallet to lie on and we'll be warm enough."

"You're not planning to stay with him, are you, Thomas?" Levi asked.

"Of course I am. He'll need someone. He's not in good shape. He might not make it through the night."

Laura sat shivering beside the boy. Was he asleep or unconscious? She pulled together the pieces of his torn doeskin sleeve and wished she had her needle and thread. She would bring them in the morning, she decided. The boy would have to hide out for a few days until the hunt was over.

When the brothers finally returned with the pallet and coals, they rubbed snow on the boy's face to bring him out of his faint. He opened his eyes and looked at them in a daze as they hauled him up onto his feet. His red hair fell out from under his wool cap. Laura walked behind as Thomas and Levi each took one arm and guided the boy across the snow-covered yard to the hill behind the house, where a potato hole had been dug.

"What's your name?" Thomas asked the boy.

"Red!" Laura answered for him.

"That's not. . . ," the boy grumbled. Then he mumbled, "Yes, Red. That's fine."

"Not surpising how you got that name," said Levi.

"I'm glad it's snowing like this," said Thomas. "It'll cover our tracks."

"Do your parents know—about the boy?" Laura asked.

"No, but they'd help him if they were here. They've gone over to old Mrs. Sloan's. She took sick late this afternoon. But it's best we hide him here anyway 'cause the militia will be searching through barns all night. They might even check out the house since Ma and Pa aren't home. But they'll be back in the morning. Pa'll know what to do."

The entrance to the potato hole was small, about three feet by two. Thomas crawled in first and reached back for the boy, who had just enough strength left to worm his way inside behind him.

Levi loosely nailed the boards back to seal the entrance, and packed snow all around to hide them from sight.

"They'll be snug in there," he said to Laura. "I'll take food out to them first thing in the morning."

"Thank you, Levi," said Laura, turning to leave.

"Wait," Levi called after her.

"I must go. They'll miss me."

"I'll walk with you till we see your house lights. This storm is getting worse. I wouldn't want you lost."

They plodded along in silence through the deepening snow.

FOUR

Laura shivered into her long wool stockings, and fumbled over her knee garters with cold, stiff fingers. She drew her short gown over her shift, tied on her two pockets, which were held by a drawstring around her waist, and covered them as fast as she could with her two petticoats. The outer thick one was quilted. She looked across the room at her sister, who was sleeping soundly in the morning light. Mira was warm and snug in her bed, not like Red, who even now might be freezing in the potato hole with Thomas. As soon as she was fully awake, Laura could only think of the rebel boy and how she would have to get over to the Mayos' to see how he was doing. She sat down and put on her calf-high moccasins. On her way past the dresser, she took a needle and a spool of tough thread from the top right-hand drawer and tucked them into one of her pockets. She'd mend that boy's clothes.

Bett was already in the kitchen, singing as she kneaded

dough on the baking table. "Help yourself to some porridge, child," Bett said without turning around. "Your father came home last night, or I should say this mornin'. He was plenty done in. He'd been huntin' down them rebels all night. Seems they had quite a fight yesterday."

"Where?"

"Down somewhere near Egremont. Their leader was wounded pretty badly, they say. Five men was killed, including two government men—and also that teacher from over Stockbridge way. Poor devil. He wasn't any part of it at all. He'd begun his day peaceful in his own classroom afore he was dragged off. But they caught most of 'em."

"What'll happen to them?"

"They'll hang 'em sure. What with their thievin' along the way, folks has no sympathy for 'em."

"When did Father come home?"

"I don't rightly know, but it wasn't long ago. He said the storm had blown out all tracks, and he'd best wait till mornin' to carry on the hunt. He'll probably be up soon, though the poor man looked plum worn out. I hope he sleeps for awhile."

Laura walked over to the washbasin that sat on a wooden stand near the back door. "He won't be here long," she said gloomily. "He never ever is."

"One of these days, your father will be home more. He will." Bett patted Laura's shoulder. "It just takes time after a war to return things to normal. He's workin' on it. He's had his own trouble, too. What with your mother passin' away so sudden, and now married again and his young wife ailin' so much, it's not been an easy life for the captain."

Laura knew that, but still she wondered about her father's part in the battle that had gone on the day before. "Did he say much about yesterday, Bett?"

"Not much. Just said they still had to find some of those fellows."

"Maybe those men have a right to rebel." Laura sometimes thought out loud when she was talking to Bett, but this time she even surprised herself with her boldness. What if her father had heard her?

"Your poor father is terrible torn up, sympathizing with the farmers 'bout here and their situation and all. Still, it's no excuse for lawlessness. An' your father's not 'bout to put up with it."

Laura finished her porridge silently. When Bett was busy cutting the bread dough into pieces for loaves, she grabbed her cloak and slipped out to the front hallway. She could feel the extra mittens and stockings she had stuffed in the pockets of her cloak the evening before.

"Where are you goin', Laura?" It was surprising how Bett could always see behind herself.

"To feed my calf," Laura said and stepped out the back

door to the woodshed before Bett had time to ask any more questions.

Grabbing her snowshoes from their hooks in the shed, Laura slung them over her shoulder and hurried out the back door. The snow from the night's storm had piled up in deep drifts against the barn and the fences. She made her way into the barn to make it look as if she were really doing chores, and tiptoed along the side of the small stable, past the switching tails of the cows. Then Laura slipped out the back barn door to a stone landing protected by the roof overhang. She stopped there just long enough to put on the two extra pairs of heavy wool stockings and her boots, which she fastened to her snowshoes with leather thongs.

In twenty minutes, she was plodding into the Mayos' front yard when she heard someone behind her. Turning, she saw Levi coming along from the barn with a pail of milk.

"Morning, Laura," he smiled. "Are you looking for Red?"

"Well, I was wondering—"

"You're too late. He's long gone."

"But he didn't have any—"

"Oh, he ate lots of potatoes last night. Then this morning, Ma prepared him a bag of bread and cheese, and a jug of hot coffee. He'll be fine."

"Only if they don't catch him."

"They're not looking for kids, Laura. Anyway, he's a plucky

lad. He'll be fine. C'mon in and have a bite of breakfast with the rest of us."

"Thanks, but I'd better hurry back. Father came home this morning, and he won't like it if I'm out wandering around. Bye, Levi, and thanks."

"You're welcome. Bye, Laura."

Disappointed, Laura plodded more slowly across the fields again. When she was still a few hundred feet from the gate, a loud bell started clanging. It was their house bell! She knew Bett only rang it if there was an emergency. And she knew what the emergency was. She, Laura, was missing! She couldn't rush too fast or she'd trip over her snowshoes. She soon reached the shelter of the barn, pulled them off, and hurried to the house.

"Laura Ingersoll, where have you been?" Bett boomed as Laura stepped into the kitchen. "Your father's callin' for you. Sam couldn't find you in the barn, and we've been lookin' high and low."

Laura flung her cloak onto the couch and started to untie her iced boot laces. "I went for a walk in the fresh snow. It is truly magnificent out there." She handed Bett her cloak.

"Well, my magnificent lady, this is a fine time to be appreciatin' the snow. Your father's waitin' in his study and wonderin' where on earth you'd gone. Now, here's your stockings." Bett handed Laura clean, dry stockings and moccasins, and hung her dripping ones by the fireplace.

Laura slipped them on and hurried down the hall and into the study. Her father, a tall, wiry, man, was sitting stiffly in a chair in front of the fireplace. He did not see her. With his head tilted sideways, he was gazing into the flames, his deepset brow and bushy eyebrows shaded his hazel eyes.

"Good morning, Father," Laura said as she spread her hands before the blazing hearth.

"A bit early for a walk, isn't it?" he said gruffly. "And anyway, it's not safe today. There are still fugitives from the battle around here. I wish I could stay home and keep an eye on things, but I must leave now to continue the search."

Laura sighed and stared into the glowing flames of the fire. She didn't believe her father anymore. He always said he wanted to be home, but he always found some reason to leave. And it had been happening ever since 1775, the year she was born, and the year the American colonies had declared war against Britain. As a rebel soldier, he had been away for most of the war.

He had been stationed closer to home when he became a captain, and Laura could remember his visiting a few times. She could still see him in his dark blue uniform with the red lapels and cuffs, rushing in the front door and hugging Mother. Then he would grab Laura and throw her up in the air and catch her. Mother was always so happy, and they would go for sleigh rides, just the three of them. But in the summer, he was always away fighting, and he was away the summer Mira was born. When the war finally ended, he moved home and Laura truly felt that this time he would stay but, before long, he was called away again.

"So, where did you go so early in the morning?" Father asked sternly.

Laura lifted her eyes from the hearth and said, "Father, before you leave, you should check in on Mother Mercy. She's very sick."

"Bett told me she had a cold but that's nothing to worry about. Just because your mother died is no reason to believe Mercy will. There's no need for you to get upset about these things. Bett and Sam are capable—I hear you're doing very well in school these days."

"Yes, thank you—and I must dress for school now."

"Don't go out again today, Laura. School's been cancelled. We've got to flush out the rest of these fellows, poor devils. Then it will be safe for school to open again."

"Father, it's not fair!" Laura burst out.

"Laura, do not shout. Now, tell me. What's not fair?"

"Hunting all these men! You should be *helping* them."

"That is quite enough, Laura. Now listen. These men have broken the law."

"Will this end it all?"

"I don't know, Laura. I hope this will stop it. When I ride out to preside over the local courts, I never know if they'll come along and lock me out. It's very aggravating."

"Sam heard that these men are only robbing because they're starving."

"I hope it's not that bad. But just between you and me, I hate rounding up these men. I don't think the law is fair. But, as a captain, I have no choice. I have to obey orders from my superiors. And now I hate to leave home so soon again, but Shay's rebellion has got to be stopped. And you, young lady, try to behave yourself while I'm gone. Bett and Sam have enough to do without hunting all over for you."

Then her father strode brusquely across the room and out the door. Laura sighed. Father never stayed home very long, and who knew when he'd be back this time.

FIVE

Elizabeth was back. Father had asked Laura to invite her on a picnic with herself and Mira.

The April sun shone on the three girls as they walked along the cow path that ran from the Ingersoll's barn to the Green River at the back of their property. Laura stared at Elizabeth as they made their way across the meadow next to the Mayos' woodlot. Why would she wear a light mauve satin gown with all the lace trimmings to a picnic? And she had mauve ribbons looped through her hair and a puffy bow at the back of her head. Laura was wearing a dark brown cambric outer petticoat and a woollen short gown that draped down over her waist. She could move about freely in the full petticoat with no fear of dirt showing. Because of her practical clothing, however, Laura had been given the job of carrying the picnic basket, and it was heavier than it had looked when Bett gave it to her at the house.

"Ooo, oh, oh, I saw one! Get it out!" Elizabeth jumped sideways off the path and tugged her skirt in toward her as if something were biting at it.

"What are you shouting about, Elizabeth?" Laura tried to sound polite, but was not succeeding.

"That! It's—it's a snake. I saw it. It was coming right for me."

"Where? Show me. Maybe we can take it home."

Elizabeth looked as if she was going to be sick. "Just get it away from me. Take it away."

"I don't see any snake. Did you notice what direction it was going?"

"Toward me! Can't you hear? It was sitting about over—"

Zing-pfff! A loud crack came from the direction Elizabeth was pointing, followed by a puff of smoke. Mira screamed and grabbed Laura's arm. Laura dropped the picnic basket but tried not to look scared. It was definitely a gunshot, but there was no sign of anyone around. All the same, the woods were nearby and anyone could be lingering there. She pushed Mira on ahead down the cowpath and told Elizabeth to get moving, too. Elizabeth rushed along so close beside Mira that she nearly tripped over her.

"What's your hurry, girls?" shouted Thomas Mayo. He stepped out of the woods, his hands in his pockets, and flashed his usual teasing smile.

"Was that you shooting?" Laura turned and confronted Thomas.

"Yes, doggone it! I missed a rabbit."

"You might have hit me," Elizabeth said hotly.

Thomas brushed his straight brown hair back from his forehead and, still smiling, said, "Awful sorry. I sure didn't mean to frighten you." He walked over to the girls with his musket over his right shoulder and his powder horn and ball dangling over the other one.

Elizabeth's frown relaxed as she smiled back. "We've come to pick flowers from your woods, Thomas."

"I'm afraid it's a little early. But next month there'll be plenty." He turned to Laura. "See anything of Red?" he mumbled.

"No...not since he left."

"Who's Red?" asked Elizabeth, stepping between Laura and Thomas.

"A friend of Laura's, from out of town." Thomas smirked at Laura.

Elizabeth stared at Thomas and missed Laura's glare. She turned to Laura and said, "You never told me about your beau."

"He's not a beau. He's just a..." Laura was furious with Thomas, for he knew how curious Elizabeth would be, and that Laura couldn't explain about Red. She could see that Thomas was enjoying himself immensely. She had to stop him from saying more.

"Would you like…to join us for lunch?" she stammered. Bett had packed more than enough.

"Don't mind if I do," Thomas answered speedily. He was familiar with Bett's picnic baskets.

Thomas and Elizabeth walked ahead together through the grass and underbrush, back toward the woods. Laura held on to Mira, who said she needed Laura to protect her from snakes. In a few minutes, they stopped at the spot where Laura had dropped the picnic basket, but it was nowhere in sight.

"I thought it was here, too, but maybe it was a little over there," Laura said, stepping a few feet nearer to the trees. A trail led to the woods.

"Maybe Levi is playing a joke on us. Maybe he took it," Thomas replied.

Elizabeth looked up surprised. "I didn't see Levi. Was he hunting rabbits, too?"

"He was still cleaning out the stables, the last I saw of him," said Thomas. "But you never know. He could have started out later. The land's not quite dry enough to cultivate. So maybe Dad let him go."

"I can't think of anywhere else the picnic basket could have gone," said Laura, "and I don't think it's very nice of Levi to snitch our food."

"Oh, for crying out loud, Laura, if Levi took it, he'll bring it back any minute now. And I don't really think he did. You two stupid girls probably just lost your own picnic basket."

Laura's eyes narrowed into slits. "Thomas Mayo! You have no right to say that."

Mira ran over and gave him a kick in the shin.

Elizabeth looked down her nose at Thomas. "That was a horrible thing for you to say."

"Well, I can see I'm not wanted here." Thomas turned away, his powder horn hanging against his side. The three girls watched him disappear into the woods.

The sun was high now as the girls looked back across the meadow. "I had planned on eating down by the river bank," said Elizabeth. "But let's go and sit awhile, anyway."

"I'm hungry," shouted Mira.

"We'd better look some more," Laura said, as she wandered back to the place where she had last seen the basket. In the trampled grass, Laura spotted a piece of blue cloth that looked like the handkerchief she'd given Red. Was Red nearby? Her pulse was starting to beat a little faster. It would be just like something Red would do.

"Well if we're going to spend all our time looking for the stupid basket, I'm going home," said Elizabeth.

Laura could barely hide her pleasure. If Red were in those woods, he would never come out with Elizabeth there. The sooner she left, the better. "How would you like to take Mira with you?" she asked. "She's hungry."

"No. I'm staying with you," said Mira, grabbing Laura's hand.

"I don't want you, anyway, Mira," Elizabeth grumbled. "Goodbye, Laura." She turned and marched sedately back to the main path.

When Laura saw Elizabeth's flat straw hat disappear behind a knoll, she walked over to the woods and shouted, "Hello there."

The sun, now at high noon, was warm, and Mira happily picked wild violets while Laura ran on into the edge of the woods. *Was Red really there?* She stood still in the shadows of the trees, listening for the scampering sounds of small animals.

"Not so loud," said a raspy voice behind her. She spun around and saw an unshaven man standing a few inches away.

"Who are you?" Laura shot back. The man was carrying a musket in one hand with a powder horn slung over his right shoulder and, in his other hand, he had their food basket. At the sound of movement between the trees, Laura turned again. Another man with scraggly brown hair came toward her. Laura thought of running home, but she did not want to leave Mira. She could not outrun these men if she carried her sister. Besides, they had her basket, which she was not going to give up without an explanation.

Just as the second shaggy-haired man approached her, Red came running up behind them. "This is Laura," he said. "She'll not give you away."

Laura was relieved to see Red, but she backed away from the men a little. "Why did you take our food?" Laura stared furiously at Red. She wouldn't mind feeding Red, but she didn't want to feed two strange men who might be dangerous.

"I went to the other side of the woods to look aroun'. I just got back."

"But your friends took our food." Her voice trembled. *Who did they think they were, anyway?* The first man settled himself down on a tree trunk, tore the white linen cloth from the top of the basket, and threw it on the ground.

"There's lots of food there," said Laura. "Help yourself. But you'd better leave the basket for me to take home or my father will be asking questions. I'll be back for it soon." She stood staring at the men for a few seconds.

The first man was eating a turkey drumstick with one hand and one of Bett's delicious buns with the other. The other man was chewing with his mouth wide open on a huge piece of white meat and a sandwich—both at the same time.

Laura glared at Red and motioned him over to a beech tree a few feet away from his rude companions. "You'd better explain yourself and those men fast, Red."

"I just found them there—honest," Red began.

"I don't believe you, Red."

"Well, they *are* my friends. I sorta told them you'd help us get food. They haven't eaten for three days."

"Are they Shay's men?"

"I'll not be tellin' on my friends."

"They are, aren't they!"

"If you promise you won't tell about 'em, they'll leave to-night, and no one'll be the wiser. I need your promise, though. And I'll vouch for you."

"Do they know who my father is? He'd go after anyone who harmed his daughters."

"No, they don't know who your father is, and I certainly wouldn't want them to find out."

"Why? They say the fugitives are afraid of my father."

"You'd be in even more danger if they knew. There's a lot of them bitter toward your father. And remember, both those men are armed. It's best they don't know."

"I want to leave as soon as they'll let us. I suppose we're being watched."

"You are that! Do you promise me you'll not reveal their identity?"

"I promise."

"Cross your heart and hope to die?"

"I didn't tell on you before, did I? And I won't tell on them if they'll just go and leave us alone."

Red scanned the fields and glanced back at the men. "Come dark, they'll be away from here, but I'd like to stay in your barn overnight."

As Red walked over to tell the men his plans, Laura wondered what part he was playing in the rebellion now, and why he had to hide out alone. Maybe the less she knew, the better!

SIX

Laura looked across the tall grass to where Mira was playing. She felt a little better as she looked at her younger sister. The picnic had turned out not badly, after all. She had managed to get rid of Elizabeth without even trying, and she had found Red again. It was strange how bad beginnings turned into happy endings at times. She sighed and smiled.

"Well, milady, shall we be off?" Red had walked up behind her. "I've set the lads straight, and now I'm after a lodging place. Do you know of one hereabouts?"

"For the likes of you? I wouldn't count on it!"

"Ha! Ha! Too late. I already have a reservation, you know. One night's lodging in the finest cow stall in the county. It says right here." Red pulled a handkerchief out of his right pocket and waved it in the air.

"Oh, your handkerchief—the blue one I gave you—it's lying in the grass, just a bit past my sister. Mira! Go pick up the blue handkerchief in the grass over there and bring it back to me." As Laura watched Mira run, she noticed that someone else was in the field. She was disappointed to see Thomas Mayo. He was probably on his way to find out what Red was doing here. It wasn't as if Red was her beau, but it would have been nice just to talk with him alone for a bit.

"Well, hello there," Thomas called as he ambled toward them. "If it isn't my old potato hole companion!" He walked up to Red and clapped a hand on his shoulder. The two looked at each other in silence.

"I've not forgotten what you did for me, you know," Red said after a few seconds. "I mean, it's not every host that lays out such a spread of spuds."

"Oh, it was nothing. We treat all our guests well."

"Laura, Laura, I found the handkerchief!" Mira yelled, running over to where Laura and the boys were standing.

"Can I keep it?"

"No, Mira, it's Red's."

"No, it's mine! I found it! It's mine!"

"Mira, it belongs to Red. Just give it to me, and I'll give it to him."

"No, no! You'll have to catch me first!" Mira started running at full speed across the grass and onto the muddy pathway by the river's edge.

"Mira, come back! Come back right now!"

But Mira heard nothing. She just kept running, right into the clump of pussywillows on the riverbank.

Laura ran after her as fast as she could, but when she got to the pussywillows, Mira was nowhere in sight. Laura looked down to the river and saw what had happened. Mira had lost her footing and had rolled down the bank and into the river. Laura screamed, but when she started for the water, her knees suddenly gave out, and she sank to the ground. Then she heard a splash and saw Red jump into the river.

Everything was a bit blurry, but Laura thought she saw Mira surface and Red grab her. Mira was choking, sputtering and hitting at Red. Laura could not believe her eyes. While Red held Mira, still struggling, they both disappeared under the splashing water. When they came up, Mira had stopped struggling. Red swam back to the riverbank, holding Mira's head above the water.

As soon as Red was out of the water, he started slapping Mira on the back. He was wet and shivering, but he didn't seem to notice. He gazed intently into Mira's face, the crease between his eyebrows getting deeper and deeper. Finally, Mira started to breathe and cough.

"Here, put my coat on her," said Thomas, who had set his gun, horn, and bag down on the ground and was standing above Red. "Turn her over and hit her again."

Red did that, and Mira spit up some more water. Then she

started to breathe normally.

"What is it? What are you two ruffians—" It was Father's voice. He had returned home in the middle of the morning, and when Elizabeth had come to the house with a strange tale about a missing food basket, he had decided to investigate. He was only a few hundred feet away when he heard Laura's screams, and he had raced ahead to the meadow.

Red and Thomas were not listening. Red was lying on his back, breathing heavily. Thomas picked Mira up and wrapped her more tightly in his coat.

"Here, Mr. Ingersoll. My friend just saved your daughter's life."

"Why...it's Mira. What happened? Well, never mind. We can lose no time. Let's just get her inside." Father took Mira, and started running with her. He was headed back to the house.

From the woods, Red's two companions watched Father take the child. They were only a hundred feet from the riverbank but they could not recognize him. The older one took out a small telescope and looked through it.

"Do you know him?" asked the younger man.

He nodded, and without a word, he handed the other fugitive the telescope and started to load his musket. "It's him, all right," the younger one said as he lowered the telescope. "We'll need to get closer to fire. When they pass the far end of the woods, the trail is almost within touching distance, and we'll be there ahead of them."

Laura couldn't keep up to Red, who was running with unusual speed toward her father. He had saved her sister, but why was he so determined to run at her father's heels? He had always tried to avoid her father before now. Panting and shaking, she sped along, hoping to catch up to her father and Red.

As they reached the east end of the woods, she had almost caught up to them. She could see Red, running between her and the woods. Then she remembered those men. Now she realized that Red was running beside Father to protect him from his would-be assassins. Red was directly between Father and the men. But who was to say they wouldn't shoot anyway?

Laura circled out into the wet fields away from the path and away from the woods. She was too far away to call to her father, and she didn't want to be captured by the men. She started running. All she could hear was her own beating heart and pounding feet. She braced herself for the shattering sound of a musket.

She kept on running and running—it seemed like forever—until she almost bumped into Red and Thomas.

"How's Mira?" Laura gasped as they ran side by side.

"She seems fine…Your father's…taking her…to the house."

Laura gave Red a sideways glance. "Come on up yourself for dry clothes." Her father could decide about this boy. Maybe she *should* tell her father about the men. She'd have to think about it.

Thomas added, "Yeah, Red...you just saved the man's daughter. He'll not turn on you now!"

They all stopped running a hundred feet from the back door. "I better not go in..." Red stared at the ground. "Please don't tell on us, Laura. We didn't harm you none 'cept for eatin' your victuals."

"That's true," she said and grabbed his hands and started to pull him along toward the house. "C'mon. You've got to get dry or you'll catch your death."

"Oh, all right." He did not take much persuading, for he was starting to shake from the cold. "Those men will be gone come dark."

"I hope so."

Laura left Red and Thomas in the back shed while she went into the kitchen. Already Bett had removed Mira's wet clothes and wrapped her in a dry blanket. The fire blazed brightly in the hearth. Bett handed Laura some dry clothes and kept drying Mira's curls.

"It's mine! It's mine!" Mira whimpered as Bett set her down on the couch near the fire.

Laura slipped into the side pantry, where she changed into dry clothes. Then she hurried back to the kitchen. Father was standing by the fire, looking down at Mira. "Don't you ever go down by the river again, young lady," he said sternly. "And whatever were you thinking of—letting her go there, Laura? I thought you were responsible enough to watch Mira. I see I was wrong."

Laura cringed and gulped before she said, "I need dry clothes for the boy." Then her legs gave way, and she sank to the couch beside Mira. She put her head in her hands and started to cry.

Father's face suddenly changed. "There, there, Laura. Don't cry. Mira's fine, now. I didn't mean to be harsh. Where is the boy?"

"In the shed, and Thomas is with him."

"Bett, have Sam get the boy a change of clothing," Father called back as he opened the door into the shed. In the far corner, he saw a boy not much bigger than Laura, shaking from the cold. Even in this wet condition, it was obvious that the boy's clothes were in shreds.

"Come in, you two. What is your name, boy?" Father had a feeling he had seen Thomas's companion before.

"Red." But the name couldn't have been less appropriate at this moment. The only colour on his face was the blue of his lips.

Sam appeared just behind Father. "I have clothes, sir," he said. Sam smiled as he handed Red a pair of his own large trousers and a homespun shirt.

"Thank you, Mister," the boy said to Father and Sam. It didn't take him long to slip out of his own wet clothes and into the huge dry ones.

"Come in and get warm. And let's get some tea into all of you," Father said. "Thomas, too."

"Well, sir, I can't stay. There's chores I'm to do. Sir, I have to get back. But thank you." Thomas went out the back door, turning to wave goodbye to Red.

Inside the kitchen, Father handed Red a towel to dry his hair. "Come over to the fire and sit right here. I don't know how to thank you for what you did."

"Laura would have rescued her if I hadn't, Mister."

"I'm a weak swimmer. I doubt I could have saved her." Laura did not admit that she hated the water and had feared it ever since a boy had drowned at a town picnic the year before.

Before long, Mira was chatting away as usual, and Laura's father did not look quite so stern. Red got up to leave. "I must go now," he said.

"Where do you live?" asked Father. Laura glanced quickly at Red, who stared straight back at her. Father saw the worried expression that passed between them. Then he remembered the red-headed boy in Shay's rebellion, the one who had followed behind the others, carrying their gear in the battle—the boy who had never been found. But this couldn't possibly be the same one. After all, it was obvious that he and Laura were friends. Mind you, he was a strange-looking one.

Laura held her breath as she waited for her father to demand an answer from Red. He kept staring at the boy, who was looking down and mumbling in an unintelligible manner, "I used to live with my uncle, but he was killed in a battle. And now, Mister, I'm searching everywhere for work."

Did her father know what battle that was? Laura could not be sure but couldn't think of any excuse and was too weak to try.

Red was almost hidden in the loose-fitting shirt and big twill breeches. His eyes looked even larger and his face thinner as he peered up at Laura's father and waited.

Father's eyes softened, and then he said, "You saved my daughter. So I'll find you a job if you're willing to work hard. Nobody wants an idle boy."

The boy's whole face lit up as he gave Laura and her father a wide smile. "I'm not afraid of hard work. I've grown up on hard work," he said. "It's like mother's milk to me, 'tis."

"You can help Sam around here for now," said Father. "Come, and I'll show you where there's an extra bed in the servants' quarters. If you've warmed up, I could take you over there now."

"I'm fine, Mister." Red was still shivering a little as he followed Father, but he turned back toward Laura and winked just as he was going out the door.

Part Two
Upper Canada

SEVEN

Laura rearranged the furniture in her father's study. She'd had to bring two extra chairs from the dining room. Father had called a family gathering. Bett wasn't able to keep up with the growing family anymore, and Laura had become a maid-of-all. Father had told Laura on the side that his announcement this afternoon was very important. Whatever it was, he was being very secretive, and that made Laura uneasy. Her father had a way of dropping news unexpectedly.

As she gave the furniture a once-over with her flannel duster, Laura remembered back eight years to that horrible time just after Father had quelled Shay's rebellion. Her stepmother Mercy had died and, four months after that, Father had announced that he was marrying Elizabeth's mother. Yes, that had come as quite a shock. Then, both Elizabeth and her mother had moved in.

Laura had been pleased that Father had found work for Red

with Judge Whiting. Perhaps that had been the beginning of her father's courtship of Sally Whiting Bachus. Laura had never wondered about his visits there because she thought he'd just been checking up on Red. Laura had been upset about the marriage for a long time. The way Father picked wives—Laura had thought Sally would probably die in a couple of years, too. Laura had secretly vowed that she would never become attached to another mother. But Sally was still well and had added two healthy children to this family—Charles, now four years old, and baby Appy who was just one.

"Thanks, Laura," said Father, striding into his study and over to his captain's chair. Right behind, Sally came along with baby Appy, and Elizabeth followed her with a struggling Charles in hand. Laura lay her duster aside and sat down on the horsehair loveseat near the fireplace.

Next, Mira came bursting in with all the energy of her almost fifteen years and plopped down beside Laura. Charles broke loose and ran over to wiggle onto the love seat between Laura and Mira.

Father didn't waste any time beginning. "I've decided to move us to Upper Canada next month," he said.

They all stared at him in shocked silence.

Then the questions began. "To Upper Canada? And why so soon?" asked Laura.

He didn't like to have his decisions questioned. "I've been

considering this move for two years."

"You knew about it, and you didn't mention a word to us!" Mira burst out. Elizabeth blew her nose with a limp lace handkerchief.

"I went to Upper Canada two years ago to look into their land offer for settlers. I made application then. I didn't see any need to tell the family, because I didn't know if we'd be accepted. And I hoped that affairs here would improve, so we could stay." He looked straight into the glowing flames of the fireplace, and Laura saw pain on her father's face that she had never noticed before.

Father put his chin in his hands as he continued. "I just can't go on here. The court decisions that have been forced on some people have been so unfair. I can't stand to watch it anymore."

In the years since Father's marriage to Sally, times had grown worse, and Father had been away more than ever. Laura and Elizabeth had finished at the local school and were busy at home helping Sally. Father could not afford to buy more slaves, and Bett was growing too old now to keep up with another baby.

"The farmers have suffered terribly," Father went on. "They've worked hard all their lives. They're honest, God-fearing, hard-working people; yet they've seen their family farms taken away to pay debts. It's not their fault they can't sell their produce for a fair price and pay their taxes."

Thomas Ingersoll talked on, still staring into the fire. Laura had never heard him say so much in one conversation. She had not realized that his work had been so hard or that times had been so difficult.

'There are men who are willing to go to Upper Canada with me. They have already lost their land here, and their hope along with it. I must persuade them they can still have hope—in Canada. Rugged it may be, but there is law and order there, and a man will receive justice. The British seem to have learned from their mistakes with these colonies."

"Was the revolution for nothing, then?" Laura asked. "Didn't the colonies fight to stop the harsh taxation?"

"No, the war was not in vain," Father spoke more evenly now. "Freedom and justice will come, but it will take time. A new country always has growing pains. But I'm too old to go through those pains. I want more security for my family."

"But Canada is still under British rule," Mira objected. She had been only three years old at the end of the Revolutionary War, but she had learned about it in school and from her father.

Father's face brightened now. "They are offering settlers a good deal. Two years ago, I travelled to Newark—that's the capital of Upper Canada near Niagara Falls—and I made a petition to Lieutenant Governor Simcoe for a land grant there.

I agreed to take forty settlers over a seven-year period. Each family will receive two hundred acres for a nominal fee. My friend, Captain Brant, the Mohawk Chief, has agreed to help me choose a stretch of fertile land for my settlement."

Father had first met the great Mohawk chief before the war on a visit to Moor's school in Connecticut, and Captain Brant had visited the family at Great Barrington three years ago. He was on his way home from a meeting with General Washington, with whom he had discussed the Muskingum River boundary for the dissenting tribes still on American soil. The chief had told Father then of the great opportunities in Upper Canada. But Laura had never once thought that the family would actually settle there.

Sally handed the baby to Elizabeth and went over to sit in the chair beside Father. She was frowning. "But the land grant is just the beginning, isn't it?" she said. "The settlers will have to break up the land, and build houses and barns, and start from scratch just like our great-grandfathers did. It will not be easy."

"No, it will not be easy," said Father. "But life never is. It hasn't been easy here, either. In fact, it is impossible now. My own resources have dwindled, and I have just enough left to take us to Upper Canada. We'll have to sell almost everything before we go—I simply can't afford to transport more. We must go. We have no other choice."

"We do have a choice. Papa will take us in." Sally suddenly turned away from Father, grabbed the baby from Elizabeth, and rushed out of the room.

"Never!" Father boomed as he stared at his wife's retreating figure.

Elizabeth blinked back tears.

"I know this is not easy," Father said, "but we must be brave. I have to get to work now. I have so much to do before we go." He turned to Laura. "Please try to reason with Sally." Laura nodded and hurried the girls and Charles out of the study. She hadn't accepted the idea herself yet, but for her father's sake, she would have to try.

"Well, I still don't like it," Mira grumbled.

"Father has been planning for two years. So it's not a sudden decision. We'll manage fine." Laura hoped her voice sounded more confident than she felt.

"I don't know," Mira began. Her deep brown eyes were brimming over with tears.

"Well, I don't like it," said Elizabeth, "and I don't know why you do, Laura, unless maybe you hope to find a beau up there."

"Yes," said Mira, "I've heard there are lots of unmarried men up in Canada."

Laura blushed. She would be twenty in September, only five months away, and it was true that she had no beau.

Elizabeth already had a beau. Now that she was eighteen, Thomas was calling on her every week. But Laura had little time to attend social events. As the oldest of the family, she was always busy.

Laura smiled mischievously and responded, "I hadn't thought about that, Elizabeth, but perhaps you're right. I may just marry a Canadian and leave you two to do the work without me."

Mira looked even more distressed, and Laura regretted her joke, but she was pleased by Elizabeth's deflated expression. "Stop worrying about Canada. You may just be surprised. You may like it there." She smiled across at Mira's shocked face as she walked out of the room. And maybe it was true. Maybe she would like it. Since there wasn't really any other choice for any of them, they had better make the best of it.

As she passed the hall mirror, she stopped for a moment. Her fine, straight features and long, thick, wavy hair told her that she was not unattractive. But she had never gone to a party escorted by a young man. Many girls younger than herself were married, and quite a few were already mothers. But Mercy and Sally had both been past twenty-five when they had married Father, so there would be time yet.

Then she thought of Red, the boy who had come and gone that horrible year when her stepmother had died. She had hoped he wouldn't go back to Ireland but, a year later, he did.

Laura had made many a trip down to the Whiting residence to see if there might be a letter for her. But there was never anything. He had not even written to Judge Whiting, except for one letter, thanking him for passage money.

As the days had dragged into months, she had finally gone to Judge Whiting to ask for Red's address but was surprised to find out that he had never given it to the Whitings. In fact, they didn't even know his real name. Laura knew that Red must still fear being tracked down for his part in Shay's rebellion.

Busy now with her thoughts as she hurried into the kitchen, she almost bumped into Sally, who was perched on a stool at the long utility table, peeling potatoes. Sally brushed the back of her hand across her eyes to hide the tears, but she kept her head down, intent upon her work.

Laura grabbed a paring knife and started to peel a potato. "You don't need to help, Laura," she said. "You spend too much time helping us all."

"Are you complaining?"

"Why, no! Whatever would I complain for, Laura? I couldn't have managed these last few years without you, but sometimes I feel that the household is taking too much of your time." She wiped a hand across an eye again. "Every girl needs a life of her own." They continued to peel potatoes in silence.

"About moving to Canada," Laura said finally, "you know we'll manage fine with the children. They're strong. And we can come back on visits, too. It's not like it was at first, after the war. Please say you'll come with us." Laura put her arm around Sally's shoulder.

"Why...should I...leave?" Sally gasped out between sobs.

"Because I need you, Sally. First I lost Mother, then Mother Mercy. I can't lose you, too." Laura's voice trembled and her eyes were misted with tears. At that moment, she realized how important Sally was to her. Though she had never thought of Sally as a mother, she had become like a very close sister.

Sally looked up through her tears, pulled back the long, dark hair that had fallen across her face, and stared with surprise at Laura. The afternoon sun shone through the window across Laura's face, and Sally could see the sadness that Laura had covered up for so many years.

"You won't lose me, Laura," she promised. They clasped each other tightly as tears fell down their cheeks.

* * *

Laura watched as Thomas and Levi helped Father load the family's belongings onto the wagon. She spotted her own small horsehair trunk near the top of the load. They would take a sloop upriver to Schenectady. From there, they would travel by boat up the Mohawk River and portage to the Oswego River. They'd end up at Oswego on Lake Ontario, where they would board a ship for Newark.

Thomas held both of Elizabeth's hands in his. "I'll come to Upper Canada one day," he said, "but I can't leave my folks right now. They need me, now that Levi has his own farm and a family to support. But sometime I'll come, Elizabeth." Laura stepped off the verandah and slipped quietly around the south side of the house.

Laura remembered saying goodbye to Red under that very apple tree the day he had come up to tell her he was leaving. Laura stood and looked at the bare branches of the gnarled apple tree. It looked half-dead today, but the day Red had left, it had been full of white blossoms.

"I'll never forget you, Laura." Red had smiled his lopsided smile, and his red hair had looked bronze in the sunlight.

"Why can't you wait just a few more years and I could go with you, Red?" Laura had pleaded.

"There's no future for me here, Laura," he'd said. "Back home, at least, I have family."

"But there are things you can do here that you won't be able to do in Ireland. You've already learned to read and write, and the judge could teach you lots of other things...and I could..."

"Don't be daft, Laura. It's all settled, and it'll be the best thing, in the end. I'll see you again, too. You just wait."

The tears had started to stream down her face then, and he had leaned over and kissed her gently on the mouth. She had never been kissed by a boy that way before, and she looked up shyly into Red's twinkling eyes. He smiled then and left her standing there, leaning against the apple tree. At the end of the lane, he turned and waved. She waved back and watched him disappear down the highway. She had never heard from him again.

"Laura!" Father's voice broke through her thoughts. She hurried around the side of the house. The whole family was all ready to go. Charles was sitting on the back of the wagon, swinging his short legs back and forth over the edge.

"Come sit here, Laura," shouted Charles. He patted an empty spot beside him. Sally and the baby were sitting on the front bench with Father, and Mira and Elizabeth were just behind them. Laura put her hands on the flat of the wagon and shunted herself up beside Charles.

"Ready to go?" Father shouted.

"Yes, all ready!"

"Get up!" The reins fell lightly on the horses' backs, and the wagon started moving slowly down the lane.

Laura looked over to the gravesites of her own mother and her first stepmother. They were on top of a small knoll where red roses grew from June to August. Laura would not see those roses this year. Nor would she see the blossoms come out on the apple tree at the side of the house.

"I don't want to go," Charles whimpered, staring up at

Laura with his big hazel eyes, so like his father's. His lips were starting to quiver.

Laura blinked back her tears and smiled at Charles as she put her right arm around him. "And miss that boat ride? You'll love the boat ride, Charles."

Reassured, he nodded and leaned his head against his sister.

Laura drew him in closer. The only home she had ever known grew smaller and smaller as the long lane stretched behind them.

EIGHT

The schooner completed its turn from the lake into the mouth of the Niagara River, plunging between the steep shale and limestone cliffs that rose up on either side of the water. Scrubby bushes and trees jutted out from the steep banks. Beyond the riverbanks, Laura could see huge stands of oak, maple, ash, chestnut, and pine. The current in the river was so strong that the ship shuddered as it made slow headway upstream.

The whole landscape was at once gentle and wild. The trees and grass looked almost like the ones that grew at home, but here they were not contained in neat woodlots and meadows. They had grown up together in a wild majesty that no one had yet disturbed. And everything seemed larger and deeper here than at home. A booming sound echoed from up the river.

"What is that sound?" asked Laura, as she looked over the side railing with her father.

"Ah, that is the sound of Niagara Falls. I travelled down

here when I visited Newark two years ago. It sounded as loud then as now. And look, the spray from the falls is just over that rise. Can you see it?"

"Oh, yes, I thought it was a low cloud."

"No, that just shows you how powerful the falls are—to send up a spray like that. I've heard you can see the spray from forty miles away on a clear day."

What a strange country we are coming to, thought Laura.

Mira walked up beside them. A robust girl, she had taken on the appearance of a farm worker. Her cheeks looked all the more ruddy from the windy, sunny days on deck, and she was almost Laura's height—five feet four inches. Laura was paler than Mira, which made Mira's eyes look even darker.

"When are we going to see Niagara Falls, Father? Mira asked.

"Oh, not today." Father gave Mira a big broad smile. "But isn't this a grand country? This is where we're going to make a new life, and where we're going to stay. Right here in Upper Canada."

"But, Father, we're so near the falls. Couldn't we just go around the bend and take a look?"

"No, Mira, first we need to get settled at the Landing—or Queenston, I guess it's called now—then I'll be going out to clear the land site on the La Tranche River."

"Queenston," boomed out the schooner's captain. He must have been as relieved to see the landing point as anyone on board. After a bad storm that had forced them to take refuge on shore, he and the crew had spent a week repairing the schooner before they had been able to continue their voyage, and the vessel was still in rough shape. They would have to take another look at her once they landed. The schooner turned in toward the riverbank. The bank came closer and closer and, finally, the gangplank was lowered.

Father was among the first to go ashore. To find temporary accommodation for the whole family would not be easy, and he needed a head start.

Queenston did not appear big enough to be even a small village. They could only see a few houses at the top of the hill above the shore. Along the shoreline stood a row of rundown huts that looked like part of a decayed military base. Laura wished for Sally's sake that they could have stayed at Newark by the mouth of the Niagara River, where almost one hundred families were settled. This didn't look like the kind of place where Sally would want to live.

The ship's captain approached them, his long bright scarf blowing in the wind. "We've unloaded your things now, Missus." He spoke directly to Sally. "You'll be just as comfortable on shore. It's a balmy day." He smiled as they left him. He did not usually take passengers on his cargo ships, and Laura guessed that he was happy to see them go. It had not been an easy voyage for any of them.

With the help of the crew, the whole family and Sam and Bett were soon standing on the shore beside their belongings.

"Look," Mira shouted. "There's a big shade tree over there. Let's go sit on the grass." The sun was shining down hotly now.

"And leave our things here?" Sally sounded alarmed.

"We can take almost everything except the biggest trunk. No one's going to walk away with it without our noticing. But I could stay and guard it."

"That won't be necessary, Laura. We can see it from there," said Sally. "Now, everyone take a piece of luggage and let's head up that hill."

Sally sounded relieved now that she was on land, and that made everyone happier to help. Even Charles proudly struggled along with a large canvas bag over his shoulder.

Once all the luggage had been carried up the hill, everyone except Sam sat under the oak tree. He had insisted on going back to guard the large trunk. Laura leaned against one side of her own trunk and watched the sailors unloading barrels and taking cargo from the teamsters onto the ships. One wagoner had a huge pile of furs on his wagon. When he reached the ship, the skipper counted them and motioned to his men, who set out several barrels and a few crates. With firm, fast strides, the wagoner walked from the dock to his wagon and back, loading his produce. When he finished, he grabbed the horses' reins and walked beside the creaking and groaning wagon as he urged his team up the steep path toward the oak tree.

Now that he was coming closer to where the family was sitting, Laura guessed he wasn't a farmer because his clothes were too neat and fresh. Yet he was not wearing the uniform of a soldier or the powdered wig of an English gentleman.

To everyone's surprise, he drew his horses to a halt right in front of the oak tree. As the horses rested, he looked over at them. His deep blue eyes were bright against his dark hair and thick sideburns, and his nod of welcome was accompanied by a kind smile that lit up his whole face. His eyes rested on Sally, who was struggling to get Appy to go to sleep.

Quietly, he stepped toward them. "May I help, Madam?" he said with a friendly smile.

"We're expecting my husband shortly." Sally eyed him cautiously. "We'll manage, but—thank you."

He noticed her hesitation. "Are you folks planning to settle around here?" He pulled his horses' reins more tightly, for they were ready to go now.

Sally nervously shifted Appy to her other arm. "Yes—but not in this area—farther inland. We'll be stopping at Queenston for a while, though."

"Well, in that case, we'll be neighbours for a while. I'm James Secord, and I've just opened a general store in St. David's, five miles away. Perhaps you'll come by one day."

Sally nodded and smiled. "Yes, we'll be needing supplies."

"Well, just ask anyone in Queenston the way to my store. I'd be honoured by your visit."

James lifted the horses' reins to get ready to leave, and gave the nearest one a light slap on the rump.

Then, before she knew what she was saying, Laura blurted out, "Excuse me, but you could help us with a trunk. It was too heavy for us to bring up with the rest."

He pulled the reins taut and turned to Laura. "I'd be glad to." He drove the team ahead a few feet and looped the horses' reins around the branch of a sturdy maple sapling.

Laura stepped along beside him as he headed down the slope. She had to walk quickly to keep pace with him.

"There it is." Laura pointed to the only trunk in among barrels and crates. Sam was leaning on it.

James took one look at the big trunk and the tired elderly man. Then he saw a wagoner coming down the hill with a teenaged boy sitting beside him, and James called out, "Hey, Josh, could you give me a hand?"

The boy was thin, but had a big smile and was willing. So Laura didn't tell James that she figured she could have helped him and Sam better than the boy. It was obvious they knew each other, and Josh liked being helpful.

James took the heavy lower position of the trunk, and Sam and Josh took the other end and carried it up the hill to the oak tree, where they set it down beside the smaller trunks.

"Thank you," Laura said, as the men stood for a moment to catch their breath. As James turned to her and smiled, Laura realized he was about her own age.

"I'm pleased to help," he said, looking at her intently. "Are you folks from the States?"

Laura hesitated and then said, "Yes. A friend of my father has picked out a land site for us near the La Tranche River."

"I guess you won't be at Queenston very long, then?"

Laura thought he looked disappointed but could not be sure. "I don't know," she said. "My stepmother would like to stay here or at Newark."

"Well, if you have any trouble finding accommodation, try Fairbank's Tavern. Tell them James Secord sent you. It's a good inn. You'll be treated well there. Goodbye now."

His horses had become restless. He loosened their reins, slapped them lightly against their backs, and said in a low voice, "Get up…haw."

The rear of the wagon was not yet over the hill before Mira sat down with a sharp thud on Laura's trunk and exclaimed, "My…Is he ever handsome! I sure hope he's a sample of the young men around here."

Laura smiled at her sister. "His name is Josh." She guessed he would only be a couple of years older than Mira.

"I'm not talking about that *boy*. I mean James."

"He seemed pleasant enough," admitted Sally, "but I don't

like to see you speaking so much to strangers." She was look-ing straight at Mira with a slight frown.

"That won't leave us many people to speak to," Mira muttered.

The sound of another wagon coming along the pathway interrupted them. Another man had stopped, allowing his horses to get their second wind.

"Just arrived from the American States, have you?" he said gruffly. He was about Father's age and a farmer, for he was dressed in a homespun smock.

Sally hesitated before she answered—the question was so abrupt. Then she replied directly, "Yes. We've come to settle here."

"Loyalists? Driven off your lands?"

"No, we're settlers."

"Settlers, eh?" The man frowned, cracked the reins over his horses's backs, and briskly pushed along up the hill.

Somewhat surprised, Laura was still staring in the direc-tion where the man had disappeared when she spotted her father. He strode over the crest of the hill and hurried down along the path toward them.

When Father reached them, he mumbled somewhat apolo-getically to Sally, "The village isn't as large as I thought. There are only two or three good stone houses in the whole place."

"Well, we can't worry about that now, Thomas," said Sally.

"Just get us into the inn. Charles is getting so restless."

Father looked at the grass beneath his feet. He couldn't face Sally's anxious eyes. "There is only one inn, and it's full. I figure we can stay in one of those empty soldier's huts we passed along the way."

The silence hung heavy between them all for a few minutes. Then Laura remembered what James had said.

"Father, a man helped us with our largest trunk, and he said to ask at Fairbank's Tavern and to tell them James Secord sent us."

"That's the place. They have no rooms left."

"Let's ask again and give them the message."

"I don't see what good that'll do."

"Why don't you try, Thomas," Sally interrupted. "This man did seem sincere."

"I'll go with you. I'd like to see the village." Laura turned to walk up the hill.

Father reluctantly started up the hill behind her. They had not walked more than a few hundred feet beyond the top of the slope when they saw the inn on the right side of the path. It was a grey clapboard building with a verandah all across the front. At once, Laura recognized the horses hitched up outside. "That's James's team and wagon," she said excitedly. Father was only slightly moved by her enthusiasm, for he was very tired and not too hopeful about this second attempt to find rooms at the inn. He had come only to please Sally.

Attached to the north side of the inn was a shed over fifty feet long, where horses were eating in their stalls. Behind them was a forest of unhitched wagons and buggies. The inn must really be full. Laura's heart sank, but she and her father kept walking up to the main entrance of the inn. Father hesitated just inside the doorway. "It's no use, Laura. The man at the desk is the same one who refused me before." He turned and trudged back out the door.

Laura stood alone in the entrance and looked around the room. Behind the man at the desk was an open doorway to a larger room, where several men were sitting around a table. Voices drifted out to her, but she could not hear any distinct words. A meeting of some sort must be in progress.

"Laura," her father was calling. She turned to go but, just then, she felt a hand on her shoulder. Startled, she turned and looked up directly into the eyes of James Secord.

"Miss Ingersoll? Are you looking for rooms for your family?"

"Yes, but Father tried here already, and they said there was nothing left."

"Oh, I see. Well, I'll ask for you if you wish."

"Oh, yes, would you?" Laura said hopefully.

James Secord walked over to the desk while Laura stayed back in the doorway. James spoke in a low voice to the man there, who put down his fine quill pen as he talked. Laura saw the man shake his head, but when James muttered something back, he nodded. Meanwhile, Father had come back inside to find out why Laura was lingering behind.

James came toward them before Father had a chance to speak. "Mr. Ingersoll, I'm James Secord. Welcome to Queenston." He extended his hand and smiled a welcome.

Father shook the extended hand. "Thank you, James. Just call me Thomas, and I want to thank you for moving the trunk for my family."

"I was glad to help. Now, I understand you're looking for accommodation. Two rooms are available with two large bedsteads, and they'll set up cots for the rest of the children. Will that be enough accommodation for tonight?"

"Why, yes," Father replied in amazement. As long as there were beds ready for them all to collapse onto, he didn't care how small the quarters. "We're mighty obliged to you for getting us a dry roof over our heads."

"I'm afraid it's just for tonight. The inn is full, but the owner is doubling up his own family to give you a couple of their rooms. Now, tomorrow, I can bring you a tent and set it up on some property I have on the edge of town. I'm sorry I can't offer anything better."

"It's the best offer we've had yet, and I thank you. Sally will be so relieved. She and our youngest are very tired from the trip."

"What part of the states are you from?"

"Great Barrington, Massachusetts, and I've come to set up a farm in Upper Canada."

"Your daughter told me about the farm. I hope you like it here. We have good fertile land just waiting to be cleared."

"My good friend, Captain Brant, has already picked a site for us, but I haven't seen it yet. I have to get the family settled at Queenston first. Now, we should be getting back. They've been waiting a long time." Father stepped out onto the verandah with James and Laura following.

"Let me help you bring your load up here to the inn," said James.

Father hesitated. "That would really help, but your team is already loaded down." James's horses were shifting restlessly and ready to be on their way home.

"I have to take my supplies to St. David's about five miles away, but then I'll come back and help you. I'll hurry. I'll not be long."

"We would appreciate your help, and I'll gladly pay for your services." Father was reaching into his pocket.

"No, that won't be necessary, and I hope that the wait won't be too hard for the women." He looked at Laura again as he spoke. "Just a minute—wait here." James turned and strode back into the inn before they had a chance to answer.

Laura noticed the relief in her father's face, but he looked very tired as he leaned against the railing on the verandah of the inn. His hair seemed more grey than brown now.

James returned about five minutes later with a round basket covered with a bright cloth. "This will help pass the time until I return," he said with a broad smile as he handed it to Laura."

Laura could smell fresh-baked bread and, peeping under the cover, she saw huge slices of cheese, a large, spicy apple pie, and some oatmeal cookies. "Thank you," she called out. He was already off the verandah and busy unhitching his horses from the post where they were tied.

Laura walked slowly behind her father down the pathway to where the family was waiting. Only once did she stop and turn to look back along the road to St. David's, but James had already disappeared. All she could see was the hard, rutted road and miles of budding trees stretching on toward the horizon.

* * *

"It's surprisingly comfortable, Thomas," Sally admitted.

While still returning to the inn for meals, they had worked for three days putting everything in order in their two canvas houses. They were pitched side by side on a green stretch of land at the edge of town, just below the Heights.

"Well, if a canvas house is good enough for the Lieutenant-Governor of Upper Canada, it should be good enough for us,"

Father said with some satisfaction. James had told them about Governor Simcoe bringing Captain Cook's canvas house from England. When the Simcoes found it too crowded in Navy Hall, the Government House at Newark, his wife had insisted he have it set up immediately for their private use.

Laura sat on a stump beside the front door to the big tent and looked out with wonder at the beauty of the steep, wide escarpment just to the south of them. The local people called it the Heights.

Laura turned toward the roadway when she heard the sounds of an approaching team of horses. Charles rushed out past her, for he, too, had heard, and they both knew that James Secord was going to be delivering the fresh supplies that their father had ordered from his store in St. David's.

James drove his team right up beside the tent and, when he jumped down from the wagon, he grabbed the excited Charles and sat him on the back of one of the horses. "Giddy up," shouted Charles, digging his feet into the mare's side.

The team lunged forward, but James had been watching, and he pulled the reins back tight. The now-petrified Charles grabbed the horse's mane and clung to its neck to keep his balance. After he had settled his team, James lifted Charles down and smiled at Laura, who had walked over to take the squirming boy.

"You'll make a good rider some day," said James as he put

the boy on the ground beside his sister.

"I'd like to ride him *now!*" Charles shouted back.

"Charles, go in the house," said Father who had come out just in time to see the boy being put down. "Thanks for delivering these supplies, James. I'm hoping to buy a team and wagon today, and then we can pick up our own supplies."

"I'm glad to have your business, Thomas. St. David's is not on the main mercantile route, and it's overlooked sometimes. Queenston stores have an advantage."

"Well, we'll be going to St. David's to buy our supplies," Father promised. "It's not that far away."

James started to hand down the bags of flour, salt, and other household items to Father and, when they had finished stacking them, Father pulled out his money to pay James.

"Are you sure you want to pay in cash?"

"How else?" Thomas asked.

"Trading at the Landing is mostly in produce or labour."

"Well, I've nothing to exchange, and I'm not free to work yet," Father explained.

Laura sat down on the stump again as she watched her father and James shake hands at the front door of the tent. James saw her there and came over but stood in silence.

Laura looked up shyly. "Do come again, and thank you for all your help, Mr. Secord."

"It was nothing," he replied, somewhat embarrassed as he

continued to stare at her. Then he shifted his cap to his other hand and said, "Please, call me James, Miss Ingersoll."

"And I'm Laura," she said, looking up into his deep blue eyes.

Just then the horse made a snorting sound and wrenched its bridle. James turned and saw the reins had become tangled in the branches of the tree where he had tied them.

"Laura..." The horses pounded their feet more. "They're hungry. I have to get them home. Good night, Laura!"

"Good night, James."

Then James jumped into the wagon and snapped the lines lightly on the horses' backs. They needed no urging to pull the empty wagon and were off at a great speed.

NINE

"Thomas, I can't believe you are going to do this!" Sally exclaimed.

The family were comfortably settled into their canvas house and were sitting on benches around the table after breakfast. On the left side of the room was Sally and Father's bedstead, and under it was the little trundle bed that pulled out for Charles. Appy's large cradle was nearby. The rest of the tent was filled with the family's everyday needs—a cupboard with cooking utensils and bags and barrels of supplies. The girls' cots and trunks were housed in a smaller attached tent. A third small tent had been erected for Bett and Sam's sleeping quarters. On sunny days, Sally and the girls cooked outside at a campfire that Father had set up and, on rainy days, the family ate sandwiches inside.

Fresh milk was delivered each day by a neighbour boy, Josh. He was the same boy who had helped James move the large trunk, and his father's farm touched the part of James's land on which their tent stood.

Father was trying to reason with Sally. "But you are getting to know people in the area now, and you have Sam and Bett to help."

Laura felt sorry for her father, for their settling here in Queenston was only supposed to have been temporary, to appease Sally until their new home was ready. Laura, too, was eager to see the site, and though she sympathized with Sally, she couldn't help wondering if Sally really had to complain so much. If he listened to her, they'd be sitting here forever in a tent instead of building a great home on an estate of their own.

Sally stared back at Thomas. "What do you mean by saying we are getting to know people in the area? Who? Tell me. The only person stopping by is James Secord, and sometimes that boy Josh takes time to visit with the girls. James has been a great help and so has Josh, but his parents haven't visited, and no women have come to call."

"They're busy. May is seeding time for the farmers, and most wives do their share with the crops and the cattle, too. There are only a few families right inside Queenston, and they have large gardens. The farm women nearby are just too busy at this time of year. Anyway, what time have *you* had for visiting?"

"I would have had more free time if we'd had more help.

Back in Great Barrington, the women often helped a new neighbour settle in."

"You have three grown girls, and Bett and Sam and me. Not many women around here are that lucky, but I am taking one of the girls or Bett with me to the site to cook meals. It'll save time for building."

"I hope it's not me." Mira was starting to look forward to Josh's visits, and lately he had dropped by quite often—even after he had finished delivering his milk. He and Mira would sit on the stumps in front of their tent and talk for ages. Father said that one day his father would show up to drag him home to his work.

"I suppose I could go," offered Elizabeth, "but you know I wouldn't be much help if I got my usual spring attack of bronchitis."

Laura did want to see the site, but she certainly didn't want to leave right now to be gone for a whole month. She'd been hoping every day that James would come calling again. He had been so helpful, and she was almost certain that he really liked her. Or was he friendly to everyone who came to Queenston? She wasn't going to act silly, like Mira, and show her feelings, but she did want to be here when he came by. If only he had a store in Queenston, she could casually drop in to see him. This waiting was bothering her. It had been a week now since he had brought the last load of supplies and stayed to chat with everyone for the whole evening. He had talked with her more than Father, but then the whole family had been there.

"And what about you, Laura?" Father was staring at her with his head tilted sideways. "Will you go with me?"

Laura had been thinking so hard about James that she had lost track of the conversation. "If I must," she stammered, "but we just got here."

"Why, Laura, that's a switch. I thought you were anxious to see the site." Father's shoulders dropped and his eyes looked tired. Laura felt a twinge of guilt, but ignored the feeling and looked away from her father's questioning eyes.

Sally was blinking back tears now. "You see, no one wants to go."

Mira was still pouting and Elizabeth was teary-eyed.

"Oh, all right," said Laura. "If you need me, I'll go, but are there any close neighbours?"

"I don't believe so. But I want to check that out."

"How long will you be gone?" asked Sally.

"Two to three weeks—no longer. A portion of the land is already cleared. Joseph and the Mohawks used to camp there in the summer."

Laura knew it might take longer than her father said and started to feel very disappointed that she wouldn't be able to see James for so long. Noticing her downcast face, Father said,

"I think I'll take Bett along to cook for me, since none of you girls seems up to the job."

Maybe that was the answer, Laura decided, and maybe Sam could go, too, but then that would leave the women folk alone in an unfamiliar place. She didn't suppose Father would approve of that. She knew then that she must go.

"Oh, all right," she said reluctantly. "I'll go."

* * *

The path beneath the chestnut mare's feet was knotted with tree roots and covered with old leaves from the previous autumn. Laura got a good look at them when the occasional shaft of light filtered through the oaks and maples onto the forest floor. The day was hot, even for early June, and Laura was tired. She did not feel very confident, either. Behind her, two of Captain Brant's sons, Joseph and Jacob, led two horses that were carrying supplies. Ahead, she could make out the forms of her father and Captain Brant. Father was wearing dark woollen breeches and a light linen shirt and waistcoat over his slightly stooped shoulders. Captain Brant sat tall in his saddle and wore an open yellow-beaded shirt, tied at the waist with a wide red sash that hung over his brown leather breeches.

Laura had not wanted to leave Queentston but had known that her father needed her to accompany him to the site of their new home on the La Tranche River. They had been away for three long weeks and were finally returning.

Father and Captain Brant had built a large one-room log cabin about twenty feet long and sixteen feet wide. And Captain Brant's Mohawk friends had come for a day to add some finishing touches. They split oak logs for the floor and built in bunk beds in three corners of the big cabin. Then, with Father's help, Captain Brant built the large fireplace in the opening on the north wall. The hearth of flat stones was backed by large field stones piled vertically as high as the wall and stuck together with hardened clay. The cabin even had one small window beside the door on the south wall. It was made from glass and putty that Father had bought at James's store.

While the men were building the cabin, Laura had been busy preparing meals on the outside hearth that was set up beside the canvas tent where they kept their supplies. The tent was also Laura's bedroom. At the end of each day, it felt good to lie there, for even the ground seemed restful, and she could hear the gurgling of the river flowing along.

At first, Laura had been very lonely, but then Captain Brant's sons, Joseph and Jacob, had come to help. They had both graduated recently from Dartmouth College in Connecticut and spoke English well. They had all become good friends, and the brothers had taught Laura how to trap small animals, and how to use herbs for medicine. She was no longer lonely and enjoyed the last week more than before.

But this afternoon, they were headed back and already things were starting to change. The Brant boys were talking together in their own language, and Father and Captain Brant were discussing political matters. She felt very alone again, just like a piece of excess baggage.

Dusk fell and still they kept on. Laura felt tired and ill at ease, especially when strange hooting sounds and the noise of breaking twigs started coming out of the trees on either side of the narrow trail.

Just as it was getting nearly too dark to see, they came out of the woods and into the clearing around a familiar small frame house. It was Captain Brant's home, where they had stayed on their way out to the site. Joseph Brant led them past the house and down the path to the Grand River, where he dismounted. Laura wanted to get off her horse, but she felt too tired to jump down. Fortunately, Father noticed she wasn't moving and helped her. Joseph and Jacob led all the horses to the water's edge. The tired animals dipped their noses eagerly into the water.

Sore from her long ride, Laura left the men at the river and plodded along up the knoll to the house. She knew Captain Brant's wife Catherine would have made up fresh beds and set out hot tea.

* * *

The next morning, Father wanted to get back on the trail as soon as possible. But Captain Brant insisted on showing him and Laura around the little settlement where he had brought the Mohawks who had fought with him for the British. The whole village consisted of only seven houses, a log schoolhouse, and a chapel. Laura wondered why Captain Brant had been so eager to show them the place. But then they came to the chapel. The high spire above its bell tower had round-arched openings in its sides, which matched the arches above the four windows on each side of the building and over the entranceway.

"Those arches would not be easy to build from planked logs," Father remarked.

"That's true," Brant smiled, "but we had help for the design from two Loyalists, Wilson and Smith, who came to live in our Mohawk valley. And we worked very hard together to erect it. Our men squared the logs, boarded, and painted it. Then they fashioned the pews out of sawn logs joined by wooden pegs. We put our best effort into God's house."

Inside, the chapel was as spacious as a meadow. An aisle ran down the middle with pews on either side. At the front in the centre was a wide pulpit, divided for a speaker and an interpreter.

"The pulpit was built in the centre so that all could hear God's message equally," Joseph Brant explained. Behind the pulpit on the wall were large black tablets with gold print. In front of the pulpit was the communion table. As they went closer, Laura spotted a carved walnut box. Brant opened the box and showed them its contents.

"This is the Bible and part of the communion silver that Queen Anne of England sent to my people at the Queen Anne Chapel in New York in 1712. During the Revolutionary War, the Bible and the silver were buried for safekeeping. They were preserved, and we were able to bring them here to our new chapel."

Laura looked more closely at the communion silver and saw that each bore the inscription:

"The gift of her Majesty Anne by the Grace of God, of Great Britain, France, and of Her plantations in North America, Queen to her Indian Chappel of the Mohawks."

"Do you have your own minister now?" Thomas asked.

"We conduct our own service. I have translated the gospels and a prayer book into our language."

"And how are your people adjusting to the new life here?"

"Well, it helps that we are together and that we have kept our own language, but our life is different here. The land on the Grand River is good for planting corn and other farming, but we cannot forget our great farms in the Mohawk Valley. Our farms were fruitful and plenteous with large apple orchards and flowing fields of corn. Many of these farms were burnt out by the Rebels in the Revolutionary War."

"But now you are settled on your own land by the Grand River. Why can't you farm your new land in the same way?"

"With what? We were not provided with farming tools and supplies for three years like the white Loyalists! So I tried to sell some of our land to get money to buy tools for our people to begin farming. They loathed the idea of selling any of our land, but when a man is starving ..." Joseph Brant stared ahead in silence.

Father said softly, "But when you sold the land, then did you buy the necessary tools?"

"Then I found out that we had not been given clear title to our land as the white men were! We could not sell any of it to buy tools or anything else. We continued to struggle on with only limited resources from our hunting. Game is just not plentiful, for the animals are being driven north by the settlers who inhabit all the area around us. My people are still in great need and some are rebelling." Captain Brant turned away then and quietly walked to the door.

* * *

In the early evening of the same day, Laura and Thomas Ingersoll sat on the deck of the schooner that sailed from Burlington Bay and would bring them the rest of the way home to Queenston.

"How are you, Laura?" Father said, looking at her intently.

"Fine, thank you. I've enjoyed this time with you, Father."

"I have too, Laura. I'm sorry I was away from you so much during the war years. But I've always been proud of my daughters and thankful for all of you."

"We missed you. Even after the war was over," Laura said quietly.

"I know—it was a hard time—to make ends meet. Many men went under with the taxes. I saw what happened to their families when they were thrown in jail for debts. It would have been better if we had followed the way of the Mohawks— no jails."

"That's right. There was no jail at Brant's Ford."

"Captain Brant had harsh words to describe our jails and the white man's cruel justice that was handed out to people who could not pay their debts. He felt the Mohawk way was better. They do deal with offenders, but they help those who cannot pay up when misfortune strikes." Father's face looked grim as he remembered incidents at Great Barrington. Then he continued, "I pledged I'd keep a roof over your heads. And I did."

"Yes, we were well provided for, and I am grateful." Laura looked away from her father's sad face.

"Sally still blames me for coming to Canada, but I couldn't live off her father."

"I know that. And Sally will be fine. I bet she's missing you right now."

"Sometimes I wonder if she'll be gone when we get back. I left savings with her. She can afford to return in better style than we came." Father stared back behind the boat. The dampness of the evening air was bringing mosquitoes now, but he didn't seem to notice.

Laura sighed to see her father's concern. "Sally would never do that and neither would Mira and Elizabeth!"

"Oh, she wouldn't take Mira. She'd leave her with Bett and Sam. But I'm afraid she'll be gone with Elizabeth and the youngsters."

"She'll still be there, Father. I'm sure, she will." Laura remembered the promise that Sally had made to her back in Great Barrington.

"I hope you're right," Thomas mumbled in a scarcely audible voice. He sat with his head bent and looked across the water swirling out behind the boat.

Laura knew her father's thoughts were back with Sally, and she felt a sudden surge of sympathy for him, and of impatience with Sally for not trying harder to adjust to their new life. They sat there in silence for a long time until the growing dusk brought the mosquitoes in hordes. Then they took shelter below the deck.

TEN

Thomas, I'm so pleased!" Sally stared out the doorway of their canvas home into the pouring rain. A wagoner was going past, coaxing his bedraggled team through the mud. "It's a wonderful idea! And if your business here at the inn is a success, maybe you'll give up clearing land for a farm." Father and Laura had arrived back from the site a week before.

Father, who was sitting across the table from Sally, shook his head.

"No, Sally, this is just temporary, but for now it seems best. The Inn was for sale at a price I could afford. So we'll be warm there for the winter, and sell it for more in the spring when we'll head out to our farm with more cash to buy supplies."

"I'll be so glad to move," Sally sighed. It had not been easy living in such crowded quarters with two small children. But now there was hope. "How soon will we be moving?"

"Sooner than you think. I found out that Fairbank's Inn

was empty and up for sale the day I came back and, the next day, I asked about buying it. My offer was accepted just this morning." Thomas avoided his wife's surprised eyes. "We can pack now and move quarters for the family. I think you'll like it, Sally."

"Really! Oh, Thomas, I'm so delighted." Sally came around the table and gave him a kiss on the cheek.

Laura and Elizabeth stepped into the large tent and shook the rain off their capes. They were getting along much better now. In fact, Laura noticed how hard Elizabeth was trying to keep up with her share of the housework. Still, Elizabeth had confided in Laura that she didn't like Queenston at all.

"Did I hear correctly?" Laura asked. "Are we really going to be running Queenston's one-and-only inn and tavern?"

Elizabeth was excited, too. "Maybe we'll make some new friends."

Laura guessed she meant men friends. When they first came, Elizabeth had gone to the Landing every day to see if the incoming mail might have a letter from Thomas Mayo. But none had come, and Laura knew how hard that was! She would always remember how disappointed she'd been when Red hadn't written.

Father looked at Laura. "I'm counting on you to help me with the books. You always have been good with figures."

"I'd like to help," Laura said. She had become bored since

returning to Queenston. The only visitor was Josh, who delivered the milk daily, but he spent most of the time with Mira. Laura could not believe how grown-up her sister had looked as she left for the ball with Josh the previous Saturday. Josh, whose full name was Julius Hitchcock, had taken Mira to Lady Simcoe's ball at Newark to represent his family, who were well established in the area.

As for James, he seemed to be nowhere in sight. Father did ask him to help move the family's belongings from the tents to the inn, but between sorting clothes and lifting bags, there was not much opportunity to visit.

Then came the business of setting up operations at the inn. Laura became so involved with balancing the books and keeping track of supplies that she hardly had a moment to herself.

Late one afternoon, a month after they had moved into the inn, Laura was sitting at the little oak desk just inside the main entrance. She had totalled the two columns for profits and expenditures, and she was worried. As she had feared, the expense column was much higher, even though they had been busy. In fact, everyone had remarked on how business was booming.

Because Queenston was the beginning of the portage route around to Chippawa and connected the Great Lakes, many people passed this way, both overnight settlers and those who frequented the tavern. Her father and Sam handled that part of the business, but all the accounts came through her books. The problem was that her father gave credit to a number of newcomers. The business just couldn't afford it.

"Laura, you've been pouring over those books all day," said Thomas as he stepped into the office in the inn.

"I just totalled the month's income. The expenses are much higher."

"Are they?" Father looked surprised.

"It's the credit you give. We just don't have the capital to last long that way." Laura handed him the open book and, leaning over, pointed out the number of unpaid bills already on their account.

"Whoo!" Father whistled through his teeth. "I had no idea."

"We cannot afford this," Laura said, raising her voice. She was annoyed that her father never could seem to make ends meet.

At that moment, James Secord walked in the door. "Excuse me if I'm meddling. But I couldn't help overhearing your conversation. You don't need to worry, Laura. Credit's always extended in these parts. Folks will pay. It just takes a little time. They're honest folk."

Laura turned around and said, "Oh, hello, James. So nice to see you again. We sure enjoyed your help on our moving day."

Then a young lady stepped up beside James and rested her gloved hand on his arm. Laura found herself staring into the eyes of the most beautiful young woman she had ever seen. Her shiny black hair curled out from under her mob cap, around her rosy cheeks, and flowed onto her shoulders. She said, "Aren't you going to introduce me to your friends, James?" She was poised and confident as she held out her hand to Laura, and her dimples made her smile even more welcoming.

A wife, thought Laura! She was annoyed to feel her cheeks reddening.

"Of course, Phoebe," said James. "Sorry. I got caught up in business dealings. I should have introduced you before. Laura and Thomas, this is Phoebe, my niece, David Secord's daughter."

Laura sighed with relief as she reached out a hand to Phoebe. She already knew that David Secord was the magistrate of St. David's and the founder of the village. Laura stared quietly back at James, who continued, "She's just stopped in for a moment to say 'Hello.' Far too busy to go anywhere with me. She has so many beaux."

"Oh, James! You do exaggerate. So nice to meet you folks. And, Laura, I wish you'd drop by to visit some day. But I won't bother you now. I see you're busy and I do have to run. Don't forget, now." Laura could see that a young man waited for her at the door of the inn.

They watched her go. Then Laura said, "Now, back to these accounts."

"I assure you I wasn't eavesdropping, but I just don't want you to worry for no reason." James was sounding apologetic now.

"It's quite all right," said Father. "Here, have a chair. You've come at just the right time." James sat down with a confident smile.

"Now, Laura," Father said, "what were you about to say?"

"I suggest we give credit at the inn only in emergency situations. The tavern should not have any credit accounts."

James interrupted. "As I was saying, you'll find folks around here are an honourable lot. They'll settle their accounts." James spoke calmly as he tapped a tune on Laura's desk with his fingers.

"He's right, Laura. I've always said you worry too much," Father continued. He gave her a pat on the shoulder and abruptly changed the subject. "James, would you like to join us for supper?"

Laura was furious. How could her father take her advice so lightly? If he had worried sooner, his family would be in better circumstances today. His motto had always been never to cross a bridge before he came to it, so he was never prepared when they did reach the bridge. And who suffered? The family. They always had to take a detour. Well, this time she'd just have to see to it that they didn't need to go around in circles.

She could run this business successfully if her father would give her a free hand. And here was James, her ideal man, giving bad business advice. Well, maybe James wasn't so great, after all.

Laura slammed the accounts book shut and took a long look at the men. "I'm going to see if Sally needs any help with supper. It's a good job that women don't wait till folks are at the table before they prepare the meal."

She marched quickly out of the room with her head held high. Surprised, James turned to watch Laura until she disappeared down the hall.

* * *

A week later, Laura was taking time out from her duties at the inn to pick wild raspberries. Sally was bent on making jam, even though business continued to be brisk at the inn, and Laura had been chosen to do the picking. She had to hold her petticoats up to keep them from brushing against the ox-eyed daisies and devil's paintbrush that dotted the land at the foot of the Heights. It was almost exactly midsummer. A grilling sun was beating down on her back. She didn't know whether it was worse to take her hat off and risk a burn or to leave it on and feel even hotter. She resigned herself to leaving it on.

She turned along the road that led west to St. David's. In order not to lose her way, she planned to keep the road in sight. Josh had told Mira there were lots of berries in plain view along the sides of the road and up the hillside on land owned by the Hitchcocks—and she was welcome to any pickings there.

"He was right," she said aloud as she spotted a thick patch not far from the road. The red berries hung heavily from the canes, and she dropped them easily into the small pail she had tied around her waist. She thought about picking berries in Great Barrington with her mother when she was a little girl. "Maybe I can pick enough for Sally and Bett to make a pie," she thought with some satisfaction. She pulled a few leaves from her berries in the pail.

As she picked and ate, the sun became stronger, and she rubbed her hand across her forehead to wipe away the beads of sweat. Three small pails would be enough to get a start on the preserves, and it wouldn't take long to pick that many.

With her pail half-full, she sighed and reached for more branches, only to find that she had picked most of the near ones clean. She would need to go farther in, where there might be snakes.

A man's voice came from the direction of the road. "Can I help you?"

Laura recognized the voice. It was James. He was tethering his team of horses to a tree by the roadway. Then, in long strides, he hurried over to her.

Laura felt the hot sun burn more deeply as she looked up at him. She imagined how terrible she must look with berry stains all around her mouth and sweat dripping from her forehead.

"I thought that was you, Laura," James said as he came closer. He reached out and grabbed both of her berry-stained hands. "You look like you've been through a war."

"Watch out, James, or you'll be covered with berry juice," Laura laughed as she looked down to her pail between them. Then she added, "Help yourself."

He took a few. "These are good, sweet berries. It must be a fine year for them. Let me help you pick."

"Don't you have to meet a boat?" Laura asked, thinking once more that James couldn't be that good a businessman if he took time off in the middle of the day to pick raspberries.

"It'll be docked for a while. Anyhow, it isn't due until this afternoon."

"Well, if you really have the time, I'd love your help. I have to pick three pails full."

They worked away together as the heat of the day grew, and the silence was broken only by the drone of the cicadas. Before long, the three pails were filled to the brim with the bright red berries.

"Well, I guess that's it," Laura declared as she untied her berry pail from around her waist. She smiled at James, whose eyes looked bluer than ever. "Thank you for helping me out. That's a hot job, and... "

"Laura, I've lunch in my wagon. What would you say if we went up the Heights to eat? You'll love it up there. You can see a long way back along the Niagara River."

Laura was surprised. Was he just asking her to be nice, or was he really interested in being with her? She couldn't help thinking how different James was. Red would have been cracking jokes, and they'd both be laughing by now. But James—still, there was something reassuring about him.

"Well," she said, coming back to herself, "I guess so. That would be nice."

James had to struggle through the raspberry canes to put the berries in a shady corner of the wagon. Laura stifled a laugh as she watched his linen breeches get caught on all the thorns. The same thing happened on the way back from the wagon, only it was worse because James was carrying a basket of sandwiches, a jug of water, and a small berry pail. He didn't have a free hand to pry himself away from the clutching bushes. Laura could stay still no longer and, when she raced over to help him, she caught her petticoats on the bushes.

"Here, you hold these." James handed her the food, disentangled himself, and reached down to free Laura's petticoat from the canes. Laura watched with fascination as his big gentle hands pulled off each burr—one at a time. In a few minutes, he had them all and was taking the food and motioning her to follow him.

James held back the thick scratching canes as she edged her way out to the clearing. From there, they clambered up the steep, grassy hillside away from the road. Weaving through the young undergrowth of oak, fir, and maple, they hurried along side by side until they reached a small, stony plateau.

Laura could see that they were still far from the top. A steep path wound ahead between the trees. James led the way up the narrow winding path to the summit, where they emerged onto a larger plateau.

"Turn around the other way, Laura, and you'll see the view." James placed a gentle hand on her shoulder, and with his other pointed to the view below.

Laura realized then how far they had come up the Heights. There lay the Niagara River far below and beyond, and the densely wooded slopes hid Queenston completely from view.

"Oh, can't we stay right here and eat?" Laura blurted out.

She turned around, then stopped abruptly as she gazed into James's sapphire eyes. "We...we can see the river from the shade of this elm tree."

"Well, I guess there's no reason to look farther. This is a superb spot."

Laura stood while he pulled the weeds and trampled the long grass, then motioned her to sit down. Before they ate,

Laura waited until James bowed his head and prayed briefly for their meal. When she opened her eyes shyly, she saw that James still had his head bowed. He was still praying—but silently.

In a moment, he looked up and Laura looked away, embarrassed.

"It always helps to know He hears and cares," James said as if answering her unasked questions. "Life is not always easy."

She did not answer.

Then, a bushy-tailed grey squirrel jumped down from a nearby willow tree onto the grass in front of them. James broke the silence. "How does your family like Queenston?"

Laura turned to answer. "Mira is really happy. She makes friends easily, and Josh visits a lot."

"I've heard he's courting Mira."

"She's only fifteen. He's just a friend. But he's a good friend to all of us. He came by one day, just last week, after his morning milk delivery and offered to help with chores at the inn. Mira had him baking in the kitchen.

"Josh? In the kitchen? I can't believe that!" James burst into hearty laughter.

Laura started to giggle. "It was a funny sight! He couldn't have caused more problems. First, he upset the fresh berry pie that Mira asked him to take out of the oven. It slipped out of his hands and landed face down on the floor."

James's laughter filled the air again. "I can see it."

"Next, he ran into the utensil rack that hung over the table, where all the other fresh pies were spread out, and all the ladling spoons and sharp knives fell down onto the fresh pies. The raspberries splattered all over the wall and floor. That's when Sally came in and sent them both out."

"I bet she wasn't too happy."

"I assure you she wasn't, but she didn't say too much to Josh. He was apologizing and looking so distressed. It's hard to be angry with Josh. I feel guilty even telling you about it. He's such a nice young man, but such a—"

"I know Josh," said James, still chuckling, "and don't worry. I won't mention a word to him. I'm surprised, though, that he was free from the farm work in the middle of the day. It's such a busy time for farmers just now...And how's Sally? Is she liking it better now at the inn?"

Laura paused, then replied, "Sally's still not too happy and neither is Elizabeth."

"It's hard at first. They're probably homesick."

"No, it's more than that. Sally can't understand why they haven't been invited to the teas or quilting bees. She'd love to get acquainted with the women in Queenston."

James looked away. The squirrel ran to a large willow tree. It scampered up the trunk and disappeared under the low-hanging branches. James turned back to Laura.

"Well, the farm women around Queenston are very busy

this time of the year. They only have quilting and sewing bees in the winter. Now they're working in their gardens and helping with crops and farm work."

"Is that the only reason?" Laura asked, noticing a certain hesitation in his voice.

"No, there is some resentment toward settlers," James replied honestly.

"Why? The war is over."

"It will pass, Laura. They are kind women. They'll soon forget when they come to know you."

"I wasn't even old enough to understand what was going on in the war. I was born just after it began."

James hesitated a moment. "I was three years old at the beginning of the war, when my mother escaped with us to Niagara. There were five women with thirty-one children. I was the youngest. We made it to a shelter at Fort Niagara in November of '76. A terrible winter. It was a nightmare. We nearly froze to death and arrived half-starved. Mother says we almost died—the lot of us."

"Couldn't your father help?"

"No, he was away fighting the rebels. He was a lieutenant in Butler's Rangers. My older brothers fought with his troops, too."

Laura looked out over the Niagara River. "Did you say you arrived in November '76? That was well into the war. Why didn't your mother leave sooner?"

"Well, they thought they might not be in danger. My father and brothers had fled for their lives from our home in New Rochelle but, at that time, the Americans didn't bother women and children. So they stayed with the hope that the whole rebellion would soon be stopped, and their men would be allowed to come home again. That didn't happen, unfortunately, so they fled across country to Fort Niagara. It was farther than they thought."

"We lived at Great Barrington, not far from New Rochelle."

"I don't really remember New Rochelle, since I was so young when we left. Mother told me it was named after La Rochelle in France. Father's ancestors came from there in 1681 and founded the town in 1689. It used to be a French settlement."

"Is your mother French, too?"

"Yes. She was Madelaine Badeau before her marriage. One of her ancestors fled from France to Bristol in England and, from there, he sailed to America. His name was Elias—Elias Badeau. Now my mother lives in St. David's with my brother, David. Father would be there, too, but he died in '84 just a year after the war ended."

"I'm sorry."

"It was an old war wound. It became infected and that... that's what killed him. He's buried in Colonel Butler's private burying ground."

"How old were you when he died?"

"I was eleven. He was never home much until that last year, but I was glad I came to know him before he died. He was worn out and disheartened. He had hoped to return to the French settlement at New Rochelle after the war."

They sat silently for a minute.

"Pardon me for talking about myself so much, Laura. I'm sure both sides suffer during wars."

"That's true, but we had more trouble after the war. Scavengers kept raiding and the authorities couldn't stop it, but when they did catch the guilty ones, they were cruel. People were hanged for stealing, and many who were in debt had all their property taken away. Some were even thrown in jail." Laura couldn't help thinking of Joseph Brant's anger at the white man's jail.

"It wasn't that bad here, except for one year, the hungry year of '88. We nearly starved. Some people did starve to death. And it could have been prevented. For the first three years after the war, the government provided food for the people. Then, just as a bad drought hit the land, the British claimed they had fulfilled their obligations and stopped sending supplies."

"What did people eat, then?"

"Pigeons, rabbits, squirrels—anything. People even died from eating poisonous roots. Not that many, but some. Most people found out what was poisonous by asking the Indians or watching the animals. Instinctively, cattle rarely eat poisonous plants."

"Really! It's good to know that's all in the past, though."

"Well, folks are more prosperous now, but they can't forget the suffering."

"So that's why they haven't welcomed us?"

"Yes. And there were rumblings again, last fall, of war with the States. Simcoe sent his wife and children to Quebec for the winter. They say he was afraid of an outbreak—I'm thankful the crisis is past—and he's brought his family back again. I suppose folks won't trust the Americans for a while, but soon they'll come to know and accept you."

"I hope so. We can't go back now." Laura looked out over the Niagara River to the distant horizon where the deep blue of the water met the light blue of the sky.

"I hope not," he replied.

Laura felt the emotion in his voice. She looked up then and realized that he was looking at her with a tenderness she had not seen in a man's eyes before. Suddenly she felt uneasy. "I think we'd best be heading back. The berries may turn to mush."

"I hope we can see each other again soon," he said.

"Yes, I'm sure we can. I'd like that."

James chucked the water jug into the picnic basket and, pushing it along his arm, he managed to carry the berry pail over the same arm. With his free hand, he reached out to Laura and clasped her hand securely in his. They climbed down the steep hillside in silence.

ELEVEN

Laura hurried to the office of her father's inn. He would have quite a few questions to ask her today, since he had been at La Tranche River for over a month. It was October now, and Laura had been running Ingersoll's Inn & Tavern at Queenston since he left. Business was good. James was right about one thing. A great deal of traffic did pass through the village.

The evening before he left, Father had told Laura that James had come to him one day to confide that he was having financial problems in his new store at St. David's. Laura suspected that he was having trouble because he was giving too much credit.

Laura remembered such cases in Great Barrington. Did some people take advantage of James's attitude to credit and his easygoing ways? He could lose everything if he's not careful! The words rang through her head.

Business aside, Laura wished James would come by the inn

more often. In fact, she was puzzled that he hadn't called on her since that wonderful hot afternoon on the Heights. Maybe he felt too poor just now to plan for a future with a wife. Was that the reason he hesitated to ask for Father's permission to call on her regularly? Or perhaps she had only imagined that he cared for her in a special way. She knew that James was kind to many newcomers to Niagara. But why the intense look in those deep blue eyes, and why had he held her hand so tightly, going down the mountain?

Laura had come to the door of her father's office and saw him sitting at his desk. He looked up from his account book and smiled. His inn was doing well in spite of his hasty decisions to start the business, and the tavern had flourished. There was a lot of money to be made, selling to thirsty men along the business route. Now he would be able to save money to buy tools and seed for his land in the spring. He thought it would not be long before he would be able to take his family to their site.

"How was your trip?" Laura asked, taking a seat in the captain's chair opposite the desk.

"Very good, Laura."

"Did you see Captain Brant?"

Father frowned and hesitated before he answered, "Yes."

"How is he, Father?"

"In mourning, I'm sorry to say, for his son Isaac. It is a

very sad case, for the father and son were estranged in spite of Joseph's many efforts to help him."

"Poor Captain Brant."

"Yes, he is heartbroken."

"I would like to visit the Brants again."

"You will," her father assured her. "We'll be moving to our cabin next spring. Now, Laura, will you add up this week's receipts while I attend to the tavern?"

Laura took her father's place and started adding up the columns of figures. Halfway down the second one, she heard a familiar voice.

"Good morning, Laura." James looked down over the counter.

"James! How nice to see you again!" She put her quill pen down and smiled up at him.

"How have you been, Laura?"

"Busy. But Father's back now."

"I see. Would you be too busy to go for a ride today? I have to go pick up supplies from a boat later this morning, but I'll be free till then."

"I'll check with Father and be right back. I'd really like to go."

Laura found her father serving a drummer in the far corner of the dining room. He raised his grey eyebrows when he turned around and saw her standing behind him.

"Laura! Is something the matter?"

"Uh...n...no," she stammered. "I just, well—James is here."

"Yes, yes, well, show him in. I haven't had a good chat with him for a long time."

"No, Father, he wants to take me out for a ride. We won't be long. Can you let me leave for a few hours?"

"A few hours! That's...I guess you must have a lot to talk about." Father noticed Laura's heightened colour and shining eyes. "Go on, then. I'll get Elizabeth to look after the counter."

Laura raced out of the dining room, not slowing down until just before she got to the doorway of her father's office. She stopped a minute, took off her apron, and smoothed her outer petticoat.

"Father says he can manage without me," Laura smiled, as she entered the office. "Where are we going?" She dropped her apron on a chair and pulled out her white lace shawl from under the counter. She wrapped it loosely around her neck and fastened it at the front with a pretty yellow ribbon.

"Well, I thought we'd just ride to the bottom of the Heights and then walk up where we did before. Come on, let's go! We don't want to waste the day."

James led her out to the wagon and closed his hand over hers as he lifted her up to the seat on front. Laura felt like an important lady, even though she was still wearing the same brown petticoat and beige jacket that she wore almost every day.

James swung up into the seat beside her. He smelled of fresh soft soap and cedar. Laura knew he must have just taken his fall clothes out of cedar shavings, where they'd been kept all summer. James slapped the reins on the horses' backs and gave Laura his big, blue-eyed smile. "Well, where to, my girl?" he grinned.

"To the Heights, of course!" she commanded. At that, James made the horses move faster and, before long, they had come to the tree where James had tethered the team that day in July.

"I have never seen anything so beautiful," Laura gasped. "It's like a different country." Laura and James had come to the top plateau again and looked out over the Niagara River, but now the landscape was a massive expanse of yellow elm and oak, red maples, with a few evergreens standing brilliant in between. The smell of the woodsmoke drifted through the air, and a blue jay screamed overhead from time to time.

"It is a different country, Laura, and it's our country now. God has brought you and I through a lot, and that has brought us out into a spacious place."

Laura knew what she wanted James to say, but was she ready yet to hear it?

James slipped his arm around Laura's waist, and she felt

her cheeks reddening as the warmth of his body sheltered her from the brisk October air. He, too, was conscious of her nearness, but as he looked down, he dropped his arm to his side with a sad smile. As his eyes searched her face, Laura saw concern there and wondered what the reason was.

James broke the stillness. "Let's find a flat stone to sit on and rest awhile."

While the thick shrubs around them were still damp from early dew, Laura found a comfortable stone that was warm and dry in the morning sun.

"How is your store coming along, James?" Laura said, once they were seated on their perch.

James hesitated and then replied, "Any new business takes time to prosper." His mouth settled into a firm line, and Laura wished she hadn't asked the question. She knew full well he was having problems. Why did she have to pick that topic?

James looked up and continued, "Financing is hard at first, and my sister's husband, Richard Cartwright, has urged me not to extend credit. He says no young business can survive that way, and that it's better to have produce on the shelves to be claimed by creditors if cash is not available."

Laura stopped herself from pointing out that that was what she had been talking about—the day James had taken Father's part against her.

"I will always extend credit to some. They are hard-working

folk who are in need, and someday they will pay me."

"I hope they do pay you back, James, and your store prospers."

But as Laura sat there quietly beside James, she knew that she loved this man—no matter what the state of his business. And besides, she could get his business in order in no time—if she were in charge. Yes, it would take her no time at all to have James on the road to prosperity. Life ahead was looking very good.

"Laura," James interrupted her daydream. "I have to go on a trip to Kingston where my sister and her husband live, and then on to Montreal...and perhaps farther."

"Farther? Montreal is a long distance."

"New York, maybe. It's a business trip. I'm leaving in the morning. And right now, I have to pick up my supplies at the Landing and have things in shape so I can leave very early tomorrow. I'll be riding up to Newark and catching a boat there."

"Oh, why...I wasn't...I was hoping I'd see you again soon."

He looked at her and smiled. "I'd like that, too, Laura, but I have no choice. I have to make the trip. I'm afraid that my supplies are waiting at the Landing; we have to go now."

James stood up. He reached out and clasped her hand, which she tightened around his. But she said nothing to James and just held his big hand.

At the bottom of the incline, the horses were switching their tails and snorting as if they were impatient to take James away.

"Laura," James said softly as they approached Queenston. He was letting the horses travel at a slower pace now.

"Yes, James."

"I'd like to visit you as soon as I return."

"I'll...I'll look forward to seeing you," Laura mumbled. She could think of nothing else to say.

"I'm not sure just when that will be." He appeared anxious and spoke with hesitation, looking straight ahead.

"I'll be waiting, James," Laura quietly promised.

He turned toward her with a smile.

Laura smiled back.

James drove the horses with one hand, holding the reins tightly. With the other, he reached out and clasped Laura's hand. He held it next to him all the way home.

TWELVE

Laura, we need to talk."

Laura looked up from the figures in her father's account book. Mira stood in front of the desk. She was quieter than usual, and there was an urgency in her voice.

"I just have two columns to finish here, or should we talk first?" Laura asked.

"No. It's not that pressing, but I've been trying to find you alone, and you hardly ever are." Mira sat down in the captain's chair and waited.

Laura rechecked her figures and continued with the next page. She was pleased to see that business was improving even more, now that spring had come. As many as sixty boats docked at the Landing every day to transfer their supplies to wagoners who travelled the portage route. Dozen of the sailors and business people stayed at the inn or stopped for a meal at the tavern. With the business doing so well, Father would be able to start up his farm that summer. Laura closed the book, satisfied to have completed her work. Then she turned to Mira.

"It's Josh, Laura," she said. "He wants to marry me in June."

"At fifteen!"

"Lots of girls marry at fifteen, and I'm almost sixteen."

"And how old is Josh?"

"Eighteen. Anyway, that's not the problem."

"Really. I thought he was barely seventeen. And if that's not the problem, what is?"

"Well, I haven't let him speak to Father yet. We're waiting for James to return. You know how Father'll want the eldest to marry first."

"That doesn't matter to Father or me. Besides, you know there's nothing definite between James and me. I was silly to think there even might be. Besides, he said he would be back by now and he isn't!"

"We could wait, Laura."

"You don't need to wait for me, Mira, but you certainly do need to wait! I can't think of many girls who've married at fifteen."

"We don't want to wait, Laura. I love Josh and I want to be with him. He's built a cabin already at the back of his father's acreage. He hopes to buy more land next to it."

"Well, you and Josh had better tell Father and Sally your

plans. Josh is a fine young man, but you're both much too young to think about marriage yet."

Mira left with a smile. It seemed she'd hardly heard a thing Laura had said.

Josh was a robust young farm lad. He obviously cared deeply for Mira, but he was far from being the rich farmer Mira had hoped to meet. Still, they would have enough. Laura was happy for her sister. She felt certain that Sally could easily talk her into waiting a couple more years.

Then she thought about herself. A young businessman passing through on the boats last week had invited her to dinner and she had refused. She was almost twenty-one now, and if she kept refusing invitations from all men, they'd soon stop asking.

Laura knew that Elizabeth had received a letter from Thomas Mayo a couple of weeks ago. He told her of his upcoming marriage this summer to a girl who had moved to Great Barrington after they had left. At least Thomas had had the decency to write and tell Elizabeth. He hadn't just left her wondering—like Red and James had.

From the hall, Laura could see a man at the counter in her father's office. She moved closer to see. She grabbed the side of the door to steady herself. Her heart was pounding, and her legs had gone weak. James Secord rushed over and clasped both her hands.

"Oh, Laura, I'm so happy to see you—so happy to be back."

"I'm pleased to see you, too, James. But you were gone so long. Much longer than I expected."

"But I explained in my letters—"

"Letters? What letters?"

"Didn't you receive my letters?"

"No, I didn't!"

"But I sent them with two special deliveries of supplies to my store. I suppose Josh or that other boy my brother hired unpacked the supplies and misplaced them."

"I received no letters and don't blame it on Josh." Laura's voice sounded angry.

"I suppose they're sitting under a bag of sugar on my shelves. I'm sorry, Laura." He still held her hands in his.

"Under a bag of sugar! That's the worst excuse—Oh, James, I was so worried about you. Phoebe said you were well, but then...for so long, there was no news."

"Laura, that's terrible. I'm so sorry! And now, I've so much to tell you. I've just come off the boat and I came straight here. Could we go somewhere to talk? It's a little cool for a picnic yet." He gave her a big smile and hoped she remembered.

"I guess so," said Laura. "No one will be in our parlour." Laura led him down the hall.

"Laura, I wanted to speak to you last fall—"

He hesitated and cleared his throat. "But I felt I had no

right…my business was in such poor shape."

"And now?"

"I've received the backing to continue with my store. Richard has helped me raise the money from friends of his. I've borrowed $800 from Andrew and James McGill from Montreal and, with new ideas from Richard, I'm confident. I'll work hard and continue in the business."

"I'm happy for you, James."

"And I feel strongly—" He hesitated and, turning toward her, he searched her face with his eyes. She could feel the intensity in his voice, and she looked up hopefully as she waited for him to finish the sentence. "—about you, Laura. I'd like to ask your father's permission to call regularly."

"I'd like that, James." Her heart pounded as she gave him a smile of encouragement.

James continued. "I thought about you all the time I was away, but I was determined to raise the capital for my store before I approached you. I'm afraid that's the reason I didn't write more often. But I missed you. How I missed you! And I love you, Laura. I know that now. Our time apart has only strengthened my feelings for you."

He stood up then and reached out for her hand to draw her to him. As she stepped into his embrace, all the loneliness and pain of the preceding months slowly left her. He whispered, "I love you," and kissed her gently on the lips.

Laura gazed back into his eyes but said nothing. She would tell him later how she had missed him. She would also tell him how much she cared for him. For now, though, she just tightened her arms around him and hoped he knew.

Part Three
Beaver Dams (Beechwoods)

THIRTEEN

Laura and James had built a home in Queenston by 1801—just four years after they were married—on the site of the Ingersolls' first canvas tent. It was mid-June of 1812 now, and the day was sweltering hot. The Heights loomed up close beside them to the south.

A green expanse of yard led eastward from the front door, down a sloped pathway of flat stones to the street of the town. A few blocks farther on, the Niagara River wound its way past the Landing. Their back door looked out toward the road to St. David's. Their grounds were spacious, and a small cabin and bake oven had been built behind the house.

James's prosperity had been recent. The store in St. David's had continued to make only slim profits; so Laura convinced him to open another store in Queenston, and it had done very well. In the last few years, business had increased, and James was able to support his wife, two daughters, and one son without difficulty. They were content.

Laura was grateful for her healthy children. Elizabeth had not married until she was twenty-seven years old, although men were continually asking her out. In the end, Elizabeth married Daniel Pickett, a Methodist circuit rider, who had come to the area near Father's farm. Laura thought he was a bit like James. Elizabeth was extremely devoted to Daniel. She even travelled with him on the circuit, which extended from Burlington Bay almost up to York. She planned to stop travelling once she had children, but the years passed and no baby came.

At last, a delighted Elizabeth had come to tell Laura the news that she was expecting a baby. Laura left her children in the charge of a neighbouring farmer's wife, Mrs. Clement, in order to go to her sister before her time came. When Elizabeth finally had her baby boy, Laura remembered the Great Barrington days. How they had both changed since then!

Now war with the Americans appeared imminent, and Laura was concerned for James's safety.

"You do look good in your sergeant's uniform, James. You're just as handsome as you were the day I married you— but I hope you won't have to fight."

James smiled, but answered his wife in a serious tone. "The talk is not good, but I can't think that we'll get pushed into war with the Americans over a battle that's not ours."

Laura reached for the supper dishes from the shelves above her bake table and carried them to the long wooden table in the centre of the room.

"It certainly isn't our fault that the British are taking American sailors right off their sailing vessels and drafting them into the British navy to help them fight their war with Napoleon."

"I know that, Laura, and they know that, but the Americans can't strike back by sailing to Britain. The American fleet isn't even strong enough to protect their own ships."

"Why don't the British stop?" Laura asked, brushing back a strand of hair that had escaped from her mob cap.

"The British should stop, but they feel the new states aren't strong enough to fight back, and they need the men for their navy. The war with Napoleon has been going on for seven years now."

"Surely the Americans won't attack us to get even with the British."

"All reports say the American war hawks are pressing their new government to take action," James replied quietly.

Laura put the potatoes and asparagus down on the table and looked up at James as she spoke. "But surely they'll not take out their anger on Upper Canada. What good would that do them? Besides, over half of us are Americans who came here long after the war. We have no fight with them. Their quarrel is with Britain."

"Sometimes countries fight their battles on foreign soil. It wouldn't be the first time...or the last."

"But isn't our Fort George entertaining the American soldiers at dinner tonight?"

"Yes."

"Well, then, you're worrying too much about rumours. Enjoy your dinner, James."

"I'll try."

At the door, he leaned over and kissed her. Then she watched him mount his horse and ride around the house toward the main street. The backyard was still except for the smoke curling out of the bakehouse chimney. She turned then as Charlotte, her oldest daughter, came into the kitchen from the front hallway.

"Didn't your sister come back with you?" Laura asked.

"Yes, Harriet is on her way. She can't run as fast, and I had to run because I knew I was late to help you with supper."

"It's ready now. Put out the silver while I get baby Charles."

Charles was already awake as Laura headed for the bedroom. Her brown-haired baby, more than a year old now, smiled as she took him from the cradle.

"Where's Papa?" Harriet asked when they were all seated.

"He's having dinner with the soldiers at Fort George tonight," Laura explained.

"Is he in the army now?" asked Charlotte.

"Only for a short time. He's a sergeant in the first militia regiment of Lincoln County, and his job is to train some local men for service in case there is a war."

"Are we really going to fight?" Charlotte's seriousness made her look older than her fourteen years.

"I don't think so, but we need to prepare. If the enemy knows we're ready, they'll think twice about coming."

"But the farm lads train for only three days a month, and now with the summer crops, they'll be too busy even for that," Charlotte protested. "Besides, Papa's new store manager says there are more than seven million Americans and only around six hundred thousand Canadians."

"God will watch over us, Charlotte, and besides, I don't think there will be a war."

A loud knock on the back door interrupted them. Laura opened it to find her brother standing there.

"Charles," Laura smiled, "you came at just the right time. Here, take James's place at the table. He's gone to Fort George."

Charles, a handsome young man of twenty-one now, was engaged to be married to James's niece, Elizabeth Secord. Her father, Stephen, had died four years before. Elizabeth lived with her mother, Hannah, and her younger brothers and sisters in St. David's, where they continued to run the mill.

Laura's brother pulled young Charles's ear as he walked

by. Charles shouted out but smiled at his favourite uncle. The girls were also happy to see their uncle, who usually had a knack for making them laugh. Laura soon noticed, however, that he was not himself tonight.

After the meal, he spoke quietly to her. "Can we talk? Alone?"

Laura left the children in the kitchen while she and Charles went into the parlour. It was spotlessly clean, filled with Laura's best furnishings. She sat on the small sofa while Charles sat in James's large wooden armchair, stretching his legs out in front of him. His head was bent over, and he was frowning.

"Laura, Father's sick," he said directly.

"How sick?"

"We can't be sure. He seems in less pain now, but it's his heart. He has asked for you, Laura."

"I'll get ready at once, but I can't leave the children until James comes home later tonight."

"Laura, he's never had the same strength since we left the farm, and that was more than six years ago. He took the loss of that farm and his dream of a settlement harder than any of us realized."

"But he's managed to provide well for the family at Government House Inn."

"Over on the River Credit, it's not like his own land. It's a leased business. It might not have been so bad if they hadn't

cut him off right away when he couldn't meet the quota for settlers. Fighting and petitioning for an extension took so much
out of him. And then the new governor claimed back even the
land he had cleared for himself. That was the last straw. That's
what really broke him. You were so busy with your own family,
Laura, you didn't see his grief the way we did. Some day I'll
buy back that land, so help me God!" He hesitated and was
silent a minute before he continued. "But I'm afraid it'll be
too late for Father. When I told him my vow, he didn't seem
to care anymore. He just smiled sadly. He seems more at peace
now, but he's anxious to see you, Laura, and I'd like to leave
tonight."

"I'll pack now. I hope James isn't held up."

"We can travel by horseback to Newark and catch a boat
in the morning, and get to the inn tomorrow." Charles looked
at Laura sadly and continued. "This has been a terrible time.
Tragedies come in threes, they say. I wonder what's going to
happen next."

"Don't think that way, Charles."

Laura left Charles in the study and called Charlotte aside
to tell her about Grandpa Ingersoll. Then she hurried up the
stairs with baby Charles to put him back to bed and to pack
for the trip.

When she had finished, she left her bag on the bed and
went back downstairs to help Charlotte and Harriet with the

dishes. She gave Charlotte instructions for feeding the family for the next week and returned to her brother in the parlour.

Charles had drifted off to sleep. He still had a boyish look about him as he leaned his head against the back of James's chair, and she was reminded of the days when she used to care for him.

Laura went up to the bedroom that she shared with James and the baby, who was sleeping quietly now. Kneeling by her bed and leaning on the soft feather mattress, she prayed silently for her father.

She was roused by the touch of James's hand on her shoulder. "Are you feeling well, Laura? You were asleep!"

It took her a minute to remember why she was kneeling beside the bed. Then she told him about Charles's visit.

"I know. He's waiting for you downstairs." James hesitated before he continued. "There's no easy way to tell you this, Laura. War has been declared."

Laura looked up at James and felt her chest tighten.

"Word came just before we sat down to eat. The British didn't want to spoil our dinner with the American officers so they held back the news until afterwards. We took the Americans down to their boats and shook hands as we parted. We know it will be far different when we meet again."

"Oh, James, I hate to leave you at a time like this, but I have to go to Father."

James knelt down beside her and put an arm around her as he spoke. "Our officers will not be acting too quickly on this news, and I don't think there will be any sudden attacks. Go to your father, Laura."

* * *

As Charles and Laura entered the large front room on the main floor of their father's inn, Sally came rushing forward to meet them.

"Laura, I'm so glad you've come. Thomas keeps asking for you. He knows that Mira can't make it." Mira and Josh had moved to the United States several years before and probably knew nothing of Father's condition.

"How is he?" Laura quickly asked.

"Not so well. The pain came again but it's gone now. The local doctor was away, and when we finally got a doctor who was visiting from York, he couldn't do much. Your father's getting weaker all the time."

"Is he sleeping now?"

"No. He knew you were coming. He's waiting."

Sally led Laura to a small room at the back of the inn on the main floor.

"It's cooler here than in the bedrooms under the eaves where we usually sleep, and it's easier for me in the daytime when he's downstairs."

Laura opened the door and slipped into her father's room. He smiled up at her as she came over and kissed him gently on the cheek. Spotting a small wooden trunk beside the window, she pulled it over next to his bedstead and sat on it.

"Not feeling so well?" she asked.

Lying against large feather pillows, he reached out his hand toward her and she grasped it firmly. She could not believe how much he had changed since she had last seen him. He was thin and pale, and even his voice seemed hoarse and weak.

"I'm so glad you've come, Laura. It's been a while now... since we've had a good visit. How's...the family?"

"They're all fine, Father. They said to tell Grandpa to get better fast."

"And the baby?"

"He's fine, too."

"Charles was really pleased when you named your baby after him."

"I know, and my baby loves Charles. They seem to have taken to each other."

Father smiled weakly.

"And how are things going at the inn?"

"Well, Sally and young Thomas can almost run the place without me now—and without Charles, I might add. He has this crazy notion we're going to have a war with the states."

"Well, Thomas is almost fifteen now," Laura softly replied.

She had noticed the concern in her father's voice at the thought of war. He would have to know, but she planned to talk to the others about telling him. Perhaps Sally should be the one to do it.

"Yes, and Sam is a help, too." Like most settlers, Father had freed Sam and Bett shortly after they had come to Upper Canada. They had moved a few miles away and had a cabin of their own on a small piece of land that Father still owned, back near the La Tranche River. But Bett had died a few years ago, leaving Sam alone, so he had moved to Port Credit to be nearer the family. He helped them with the daily chores.

"How is Sam?"

"He has been well. But last week…he took sick. Could be the smallpox. Folks are afraid to go near him."

"Who's taking care of him?"

"The boys leave milk and food in front of his cabin. He keeps getting his food, so he's managing. I do have lots of help around here. Even young James is energetic. He'll be twelve soon."

"You must be proud of all your sons, Father."

"Yes, but my daughters, I'm proud of them, too. They'll always mean as much to me, especially my firstborn." He squeezed her hand and added, "Our little Sarah is a handful. I think the older ones are spoiling her."

"I don't think Sally will let that happen."

"You look so much like your mother, Laura. So many years ago—but sometimes I remember her as if it were yesterday."

"Perhaps I look like her, but the family say I'm more like you."

Father chuckled. He seemed pleased to hear her say that. Feeling a little stronger, he sat up. Laura pushed more feather pillows behind him for support.

"This inn does keep us busy," he said, brightening some more. "We have all types of people here, Laura. The governor stops here. The traders come on horseback from the north, and people sailing from the east come to this end of the lake. Most times, I enjoy their tales, but there's been talk of war lately. I can't see it happening, though. We've all got relatives on the other side. At this job, I've learned not to pay too much attention to what I hear. I wish Charles would follow that advice." Father was becoming breathless now.

Laura tried to change the topic. "I hear you have a reputation as a fine host. People enjoy their stopover at this inn."

"The family have been carrying on very well without me lately, but I think I'll be up soon. Just talking to you like this is raising my spirits." Laura smiled and rubbed her warm hand over her father's thin one.

Father began to look tired again and rested heavily against the pillows. They sat there silently. Then he spoke. "It's getting late, Laura, and you must be tired. If you would just bring me a glass of water, I'll settle down for the night. We'll have a great long visit in the morning."

"I can stay a while, so we'll have lots of time to visit," Laura said. Actually, she wondered how long she could really stay with the threat of war over all of Upper Canada. James would have to defend Queenston if the Americans attacked, and she would have to go back to be with the children. Still, she could not worry her father with that news tonight. She would have to talk it over with Sally in the morning.

Laura made her father as comfortable as possible for the night and went for the water. When she returned, he was lying very still, and she thought he was asleep. She set the water down on the night stand and tiptoed to the door.

"Laura ..." her father said softly in his raspy voice.

"Yes, Father."

"Thank you for coming. We'll have a good visit in the morning. I think I'll get up then. It's time I was getting about again."

"I'm looking forward to that. Good night, Father."

Laura went up to a small room under the eaves that Sally had prepared for her, and quickly got ready for bed. She was very tired from the hurried journey and from the strain of the war news. How could she possibly tell her father?

And she worried about her children, so far from her. If Lake Ontario was blockaded, she would have to take the longer journey home overland, and no one knew where the Americans would strike. James had said four main areas were possible targets: Amherstburg on the southern tip of Lake Erie, Kingston, Montreal, and their own Queenston. As a centre of the portage route, Queenston was in a strategic position.

At the side of the bed, she knelt and prayed that her father would face the news of war, and that her children and James would be safe. She was thankful she had been able to see her father again. When at last she climbed into bed, she sank deep into the feather mattress and fell asleep almost at once.

Laura awakened early, as usual, to see beams of light streaming through the small open window across the foot of her bed. The morning air was much cooler than it had been the day before. She got up and dressed quickly and walked into the hall. A pitcher of fresh water was already sitting outside her door. Someone must have been up before sunrise. Feeling grateful that she did not have to go down to the pump, she took the water back to her room and washed up.

When Laura walked into the kitchen, Sally was already there, stirring porridge. She looked older now—wisps of grey hair hung loosely about her face. Laura wondered how she kept up so well at fifty-one, with five-year-old Sarah and all the work of the inn, now that her husband was too sick to help. Sally had certainly not had an easy time since they had come to Canada, but she had accepted the life here and grown to like it.

"How's Father?" Laura asked as Sally turned to greet her.

"I believe he had a good night. I looked in on him several times. I didn't want to disturb him. He was lying very still."

"He says he'll be getting up today."

"I hope he'll be careful if he does," Sally said as she sliced bread on her cutting board. "Laura, please advise me. I don't know how long I can keep the news of the war from Thomas. People come by all the time. They'll be talking of nothing else. And Charles left early this morning. He's been called to active duty. How can I tell your father?"

Laura felt at a loss for words. "I don't know," she said finally.

"Well, I need to know now," Sally said even more anxiously. "I can make an excuse for Charles going, but if Thomas gets up today, he's bound to hear the news. It'll be hard on him, Laura."

"It'll be easier if he learns it from us. Maybe we should both tell him."

"You're right, Laura."

Sally dished out two bowls of oatmeal porridge topped with maple sugar, and they ate in silence. "May I help prepare breakfast for your guests?" Laura asked when they had finished.

"No, I'll wake Appy. She'll take care of that. You could check on your father, though. I haven't looked in on him since I got up quite early this morning."

Laura slipped into the narrow hallway and walked along to

her father's room. His door was ajar and he was lying very still with his back to the door. She heard a gurgling sound just as she came into the room. She tiptoed across to the bed.

Her father's face was very, very pale. His eyes were closed.

Laura recognized the death-like whiteness that masked his face, and she spoke to him. "Father. Father." He did not answer.

Nor did he ever answer again.

Even in her grief, Laura was thankful that her father never had to face the news of the war.

FOURTEEN

A day after the funeral, Sally and Laura sat in silence on the back steps of the inn. As the evening shadows fell across them, Sally turned to Laura, her eyes still red from crying, and said softly, "My children are still with me, Laura, and I will manage. You must go now to yours."

Laura knew she was right, for the fear of war hung over all of them. "I will go tomorrow," she said, "but first I want to see Sam."

Just then, young Thomas came by, and Laura felt a twinge of pain as he looked at his mother with his head tilted sideways. It was the way Father used to hold his head when he had something serious to say. "Sam did not pick up his food today," he said.

"I must go to him," Laura said. "He'll need help." They both knew that he must be very sick if he could not make it just outside his door for the food.

"But the smallpox!" Sally exclaimed. "Don't take Thomas. I can't have any more sickness just now." She started to sob into her apron.

"I'm not afraid," Laura said. "I'm immune, and he may need care."

"How can you be sure that you won't take the disease?" asked Thomas.

"I've had cowpox," said Laura.

"I know they say that cowpox protects you from smallpox," said Sally, "but I've known folks who've had cowpox and took the disease anyway."

"Well, I won't. I've cared for many in our area with the smallpox when no one would go near them. Neither I nor my family have suffered. I'm careful, of course. I use lots of soft soap and hot water."

"You can't be too careful around smallpox."

"Has the doctor visited?"

"No, and I understand that he is immune, too, and goes regularly into houses with the smallpox. But Thomas asked him to visit Sam and he refused."

"Why?"

"Because Sam's black. The doctor was determined not to go, and Thomas was just too weak to argue."

"Well, I'm not," Laura said indignantly. She stood up and straightened out her long petticoat. She pushed back a few strands of loose hair behind her mob cap and left Sally and young Thomas sitting on the steps. She hastened along the pathway to the doctor's house, not far from the inn.

She had intended to pay this visit sooner, but she knew Sally would worry about her carrying the illness to the family. So she had planned to pack everything now and visit Sam on her way back home. But this sudden news about his food left her no choice.

The doctor's house was the largest in the small village, and Laura walked briskly up the front steps and knocked on the door. A middle-aged woman servant with a white apron over her petticoats opened the door and stared out silently.

Laura pushed back the open door and stepped inside. "I'm Thomas Ingersoll's daughter, and I've come to see the doctor. Please tell him I'm here."

The woman nodded with a look of recognition and respect, and motioned Laura to follow her down the hall to an open door. Laura entered and saw that the doctor was seated before his desk and was busy writing. He did not look up until he had finished the line. Then he started to speak even before his eyes left the page. "I am sorry about Thomas," he said. "He was a fine man, but I did all I could."

"I know that, thank you. I am not here about my father."

"Are you not well? I could give you some powders for sleep."

"It is not myself. I'm here about Sam. I understand that

you are immune and do not hesitate to visit those with smallpox."

The doctor's face hardened. "I was too busy to visit him when your father mentioned it. I'll drop by there tomorrow sometime."

"I fear that may be too late, for he did not pick up his food today," Laura continued. "Obviously he is too sick to go those few steps. He may even be unconscious."

The doctor laid his pen onto his writing paper and looked up impatiently. "Oh, very well. If I must, I'll go tonight."

Laura walked back to the inn, uneasy still about the doctor's tone. She would have to go to Sam's herself, to make sure the doctor kept his promise. She would pack now, and her bags would be ready for Thomas to pick up, so she would not need to return to the inn.

Half an hour later, with only one small bag, she hurried in the moonlight along the grassy pathway to Sam's. She had changed into an old petticoat and jacket, which she would leave behind so that she would not carry the disease. Inside her small bag, she carried a complete change of clothing for her return trip, and a bar of Sally's soft soap, heavy with lye.

As Laura reached the back of Sam's house, she recognized the doctor's horse and buggy tied to the back post. "Good!" she thought. "At least he's come promptly. His bark must be worse than his bite." With a sigh of relief, she quietly set down her bag on the stone stoop, lifted the latch on the back door and stepped inside.

She stood staring in silence at the sight before her. Across the room, the doctor was bent over Sam's small cot, holding a large feather pillow over Sam's face.

"Stop!" screamed Laura, rushing to the doctor.

The doctor turned in surprise and jerked the pillow away. "What good is he?" he snarled at Laura. "He's not of much account anyway and will only spread the disease. Not too many people are immune as we are. I'll finish him off now while he's unconscious and get someone here to bury him and his sores. Look! He's a mass of infestation."

Laura knew she did not have the physical strength to stop the doctor, but she would use the talent she did have, her sharp tongue. "As sure as you do, I will have you indicted for murder," she answered hotly.

The doctor looked up at her as she stood there, unflinching. His eyes were beady lights in the dimness of the room. They stared at each other, with the sound of Sam's heavy breathing between them. Finally, the doctor put the pillow down beside Sam. Turning from the bed, he said, "Well, if we must save him, we'll have a heavy night ahead, for without help, he'll suffocate from the pneumonia before morning. First, we need fresh water."

With relief, Laura lit a candle and placed it on the small

table beside the bed. Then she ran out to the well, which was only about ten feet away from the back door, and let down the empty pail until she heard the splash as it hit the bottom. She lost no time rolling it up and pulling it out of the well. Would the doctor change his mind while she was gone and attack Sam again? In her hurry, as she ran along the pathway, the water splashed out of the pail against her petticoat, and she was breathless when she stepped inside. She was glad to see the doctor busy mixing powders. He must have taken her threat seriously.

Laura started a small fire in the fireplace in the front room of the cabin, then filled two pans with water to boil. Peering under the mat in front of the hearth, she saw the trap door. In a moment, she had lit a candle from beside the fireplace, pulled up the door, and slipped down the ladder into the darkness. When she reached the dirt floor, she could see the piles of vegetables that Sam had stored there the fall before. When she came to the onions, she filled a large pan, and was about to climb up the ladder when she heard footsteps just above her. She heard the horses neighing outside and the doctor shouting. Was he leaving? Had he closed the door over the hole to the cellar? She stuck the candle into her pan of onions and hurried up the ladder, clutching the side with her free hand and hoping that her head would not bump against the dropped trap-door.

The entrance was the same as she had left it. Hurrying into Sam's room, she saw he was alone, his eyes still closed. She set the onions on the table and went to the door. The doctor was coming back inside.

"I've left more powders on the table," he said. "Mix them for him every few hours. If he regains consciousness, put them in his tea. They'll help the fever and pain. And get some rest yourself." He motioned to the other cot across the room. "I'll be back in the morning." He turned then and left without further explanation.

Laura went out on the back step to peel the onions. She was making a pack for Sam's chest to help relieve the congestion. She thought back to the days in Great Barrington when Sam and Bett had always been there when Mother and Mercy had been sick and Father was away. She was glad she could be here now, but she felt so alone and longed for her children. What if the fighting started and she could not reach them?

After she finished her peeling, she rummaged around Sam's room for an old stocking, filled it with steaming onions, and placed it on Sam's chest. Then she went out to the back stoop to get some fresh air.

As she leaned against the corner post, she prayed that Sam would soon be well enough to manage. And that they would be kept safe back home.

* * *

A week later, Sam had recovered enough to care for himself, and Laura returned to Queenston. She had not had much time to think of her father. Her grief was still fresh. Back in Queenston, though, she was comforted by her own children and by James, all active and healthy.

The summer days of 1812 were warm and mellow and the crops flourished, but Laura and James and everyone else who lived near Queenston thought of nothing but war. They wondered, at the beginning of each new day, whether it would be the one to bring disaster. James spent all his time at the Queenston barracks now, training local men for an emergency. Most of the locals were farmers, however, and were reluctant to leave their farms at this busy time of the year. James felt they were not taking the war seriously enough.

Then the unbelievable news began to arrive. An American brigadier-general, William Hull, had led troops across the Detroit River into Upper Canada. By the middle of July, he had sent men out to plunder the countryside, but he never did manage to attack Amherstburg's Fort Malden. British scouting parties took his supply trains, and a British schooner seized even his camping plans. In mid-August, he retreated across the Detroit River.

Everyone gave the credit to the commander of the Upper Canada troops, Isaac Brock, who, with great daring, had chased the Americans to Fort Detroit and demanded their surrender.

His boldness was rewarded, and he obtained a generous supply of much needed weapons and stores for Canada. The news was not all good, however. It seemed obvious now that the next attack would occur farther east. Would it be at Queenston?

"The local fellows are taking this war more seriously now," James told Laura one day in September. Then he added thoughtfully, "We all are."

Laura stocked their cold cellar well. During the fall, she stored twice as many supplies of root vegetables and fruits. As usual, she stored turnips, potatoes, russet apples, sugar pears, dried peaches, cherries, and berries—and the plums—Blue, Damson, Green Gage, and Egg.

James had insisted that they keep Fan and Bob, the black servants he had hired while Laura had gone to see her father. They were a great help putting up the extra preserves. James had dug out an additional hidden back room behind and under the regular fruit cellar, disguising the entrance with a trap door hidden under the sod. Food could be scarce in war time, and he didn't want any of their supplies stolen.

In early October, James returned from military duty one day with the news that Brock was expecting an attack along the Niagara River. Queenston seemed a likely place, since it was so close to the American side. Newark and Fort George, where Isaac Brock had stationed his men, were also on the alert.

James, a sergeant in the First Lincoln Militia, kept watch

with his volunteers around the clock. Laura watched him leave with some anxiety and prayed for strength to face whatever lay ahead.

FIFTEEN

Laura woke up with a start. She was almost certain she had heard the sound of a cannon firing. So, it had begun. The war they had all dreaded had come to Queenston and Niagara.

Laura jumped from her bed and hurried to the window to look out. She could see nothing but rain pelting against the window in the jet blackness of the October night.

James, where are you? she asked herself. *Are you at the Landing to meet the enemy or have you gone to Fort George? Or maybe you're with General Brock.* She prayed aloud, "Please, God, protect him wherever he is."

"Mama, mama." The cry came from the cradle beside the bed as her son, Charles, woke up in fear.

Harriet and Charlotte stumbled into the room, almost tripping on their long flannel nightgowns. "Is that gunfire, Mama?" asked Harriet, still rubbing her eyes.

Charlotte was fully awake and asked anxiously, "Is it a

bad thunderstorm? Do you want us to go downstairs?" But Laura could see the fear in her eyes and realized that her oldest daughter was well aware of the danger ahead.

"You go back to sleep now—all of you," Laura said. "I'm keeping watch and, if I need to, I'll call you." Reassured, they returned to their beds.

Laura sank to her knees and leaned against the bed until the thumping of her heart had eased. After a short time, she got to her feet and dressed quietly, putting on her old short gown and petticoats. She lay back on the bed, fully dressed, and listened to the heavy rain.

It was still dark when Laura roused herself from a half-sleep. She looked down at Charles, who had kicked away his covering. His chubby pink toes lay bare on the quilt. Laura got up and pulled the blanket back over him, for the chill of the storm had penetrated the house. The clock on the dresser struck five a.m. It was time to get the girls ready to leave the house.

In the girls' room across the hall, Charlotte was lying with her eyes wide open, but Harriet was sleeping soundly in her bunk opposite the bedstead. Laura cautioned Charlotte with a finger to her lips and pointed to the clothes on the bedpost, then she walked out of the room and went downstairs.

When Laura entered the kitchen, she was surprised to see Bob and Fan already moving around. Bob had a crackling fire going in the fireplace, and Laura stood by the hearth to warm herself. Fan was shaking as she stirred the porridge in the iron pot over the hearth. "Why can't them Americans just stay home, anyway? We don't want their laws here."

Bob and Fan had come from the settlement of former slaves on the southwest side of St. David's. They, and many others who lived there, had been freed under a law passed by Governor Simcoe in 1793. The new legislation forbade the import of slaves into the province and freed the children of slaves when they reached the age of twenty-five. It was no wonder that Fan feared an American takeover. It could mean she and her husband would be sent back to slavery.

After Laura helped prepare the breakfast, she went out the back door of the house and looked up to the Heights. It was still dark, but the rain was falling less heavily now. She could hear rustling sounds. Was there movement between the trees? She shrank back in fear to the side of the house and strained to see.

A bolt of lightning streaked across the sky and, in its pale light, she saw men in the red uniform of the British Army walking up the hill on foot. There was a great clap of thunder and, at the very same moment, the firing of guns.

Laura ran into the house and up the stairs and took a deep breath outside her daughters' room. Then she went in and spoke with a quiet firmness that did not reveal her fear. "Harriet, dress quickly, and Charlotte, please get the baby ready." Laura had trained her children before the crisis, and they knew now that they must do exactly as she said.

But before they could go down the stairs, they heard men's voices and a loud banging at the back door. All four froze in fear as Laura called out, "Who is it?"

The voices were not distinguishable at first. Then they heard James above the noise of the others. "It's me, Laura."

While the children huddled together at the top of the stairs, Laura ran down to the door and pulled up the latch lock.

James burst into the room with three other men. Their red jackets and white breeches were soaking wet and spattered with mud. The sickening smell of wet wool and blood filled the hallway. The four of them carried a very large man in a gold-trimmed scarlet uniform. Laura held up a candle and, in its flickering light, she saw that the officer's chest was soaked in blood.

"Quick, Fan," Laura whispered as she stared at the wounded man. "Bring water and cloths."

Her husband's face was ashen, for the man they carried was their own General, Isaac Brock. "Up the stairs," gasped James, his arms under one shoulder of his commander.

The frightened children scurried back to their room, and Laura handed Charles over to Charlotte. She closed their door tightly behind her as the men climbed the stairs very slowly with their precious burden.

The door to her bedroom was still open when she left the

girls, and she could see the men by the bed, bending over the general. James came out alone to her and closed the door behind him.

"Laura, General Brock cannot be helped now. Tell Fan not to bring the water. In case the body is found here, we are removing his uniform so he can't be identified by the enemy. We do not want them to know our leader is dead; nor do we want them to have the body. They'll not recognize him out of uniform."

"What are we to do—the children, James?"

"Go to the country. There is still some cover of darkness. Go through the village to the north side and then straight west. You'll be safe there. For now, the Americans want Queenston. The countryside is safe."

"But where are they? I thought the fighting would be at the Landing."

"We thought so, too. We had it well guarded, but somehow they found a way to the Heights up the sheer cliffs through the fishermen's pass. Only a few from Niagara know that way. Someone has betrayed us."

"Where are the general's men?"

"They aren't here yet. When General Brock heard the cannon, he thought it was a ruse to draw his men away from their stronghold at Fort George so the enemy could attack there. He didn't believe it was possible for them to find their way, let alone to climb that cliff. He felt the real fighting would come at the Landing, and he knew we were well prepared to hold out there until he could bring his men. So he left his men and came himself to investigate the situation."

"It must have been three in the morning when I heard that cannon. Did the sound come from across the river?"

"No, it was our own cannon stationed halfway up the Heights above Queenston. Our men shot it to warn us, then spiked it, making it useless, and fled down the hill. They never reached the bottom because the warning sound revealed their position and they were shot."

"Why didn't General Brock wait for more men before he attacked?"

"If he'd waited, he wouldn't have been able to stop the Americans from marching in and taking Queenston. We held them back, and Colonel Macdonell should be here any minute to lead the next attack. The Americans have retreated for the moment."

The solemn-faced soldiers hurried out of the bedroom, and James said, "I must go, Laura. You and the children hurry away. Bob and Fan will help."

James and the other men rushed down the stairs and were gone.

"Come quickly," Laura called to her children, opening their door. They crowded behind her as they went down the stairs.

Bob and Fan, who were waiting in the hall, helped put a cape on Charles, and they all hurried outside. The raw, wet wind cut through them as they walked along the street leading away from the Heights.

It seemed to take forever to reach the north end of town. It had started to rain again when they got there, and they met scores of wet and dirty Canadian and British soldiers marching down the main road toward them. Bob cheered loudly when Captain Runchey's company of black soldiers came into sight.

The family turned up a side street, then headed north and west. Before long, they were on the outskirts of Queenston.

"We'll cut across country now," said Laura. She knew that any farm family would take them in, but the farther they went from Queenston, the safer they would be. She decided to head for the Chrysler or Clement farm.

They walked on in broad daylight now, and the rain had almost stopped. A silly rhyme that her father used to repeat started ringing in Laura's ears: "If it rains before seven, it'll stop before eleven." Barely four months had passed since his death and she thought of him often. But if he were alive now, he would surely be grieved by this war. How torn he would have been, for he had friends on both sides.

The sound of gunshots echoed from the Heights behind them. Looking back, she could see flashes of gunsmoke. God, please keep James safe, she pleaded silently as she pushed along.

"Aren't we ever gonna get there?" Harriet grumbled.

"How about a ride?" Bob asked, lifting the small girl onto

his broad shoulders. From her new perch, Harriet smiled at the others who were still walking.

"May I carry Charles a piece, Ma'am?" Fan asked.

"I'll be all right. He's asleep, and it's not far now." Laura's arms did ache, though, for Charles was a big baby. Laura turned to look back and saw other groups of women and children coming from the southeast.

The road was muddy in places, and as they reached the woods near the back of Clements' farm, she said, "Climb through this rail fence here, and we'll cut off at least a mile from going on the road." They all squeezed through between the rails and pushed along a trail through the bush. The grass along the edges was long and very wet, but at least they were free of the mud on the road.

Finally, they saw the big grey, flat-board barn and the log cabin beyond. As they approached the house, Mrs. Clement swung the door wide open and reached out for the baby. Her usually jolly face was sober as she laid Charles on the bed in the adjoining room.

Pale-faced, the girls huddled together on the long bench by the hearth. The fire felt good.

"Will you have some porridge for yourself and the young-uns?" asked Mrs. Clement. "It'll warm you."

"We'll just rest first, thank you," Laura said, collapsing into a chair before the fire.

Mrs. Clement nodded and turned to stir the big pot of oatmeal porridge that she had already prepared for any who might come that day.

* * *

Much later in the morning, as Laura cut bread for the noon meal and the children played outside, she heard a loud knock at the front door. She went to open it and was not surprised to see Mrs. Law, another woman fleeing from Queenston, along with her eleven-year-old son, John. The Laws lived across town from the Secords, but they had chatted many times in the Secords' general store.

"We've just come from Queenston," she said. Her face had lost all of its colour and, glassy-eyed, she mumbled, "The fighting is bad. My husband and older son have been killed in the battle. I fear the Americans will take Queenston."

Her red-headed son, John, stared straight ahead, too, and sat down silently on a chair just inside the door. He did not look like his usual self at all, with his face so pale even the freckles were faded. The stubborn expression on his face and his wild-looking hair reminded Laura of someone.

"Mama, Charles is crying," Charlotte called from the bedroom. Laura went in to calm the baby and to coax him to eat a little.

When she came back into the kitchen, Mrs. Clement, Fan, and Charlotte had set the table for all of them. It was a simple meal of bread, turnips, and fried pork, with a glass of milk for each child.

"I'll call the others," Laura said, going to the door. Her children came running to the house, but young John Law was not with them.

Mrs. Law, who had sat in a numbed state on the kitchen couch since her arrival, suddenly came to life, screaming, "Where's my son?" She stared wildly about and then rushed out of the house.

Laura looked at Mrs. Clement, who gave her a knowing glance. The woman had just lost her husband and older boy that morning. No wonder she was panicking. Laura suddenly realized whom young John had reminded her of. He looked just like Red, that unforgettable fugitive from a different battle. But now, she and her children were the fugitives.

"We must all help her look," Laura said, breaking off her thoughts. The older children raced outside to hunt while Laura and Mrs. Clement started searching through the house.

"More than likely he's crawled into a corner in the barn somewhere. That young'un is havin' hisself a good cry where no one cin see him," Mrs. Clement said.

Laura was looking behind the barrels on the back stoop when she noticed the elderly Mr. Clement heading toward the house.

"Was he in the barn?" Mrs. Clement asked anxiously, coming up behind Laura.

"No, but since you've not found him, I cin go back and check agin."

Mr. Clement turned to go back to the barn, but stopped abruptly at Mrs. Clement's cry. "Joseph, your musket's missin'—and your cartridge pouch, too! Don't you always keep 'em in back of the pantry?"

'Yep, haven't moved them for weeks."

Laura and Mrs. Clement knew they must tell the boy's mother.

Mrs. Law came quickly, her eyes red from crying, but she looked hopeful as she searched their eyes for confirmation that her son was found.

"My husband's musket and box of cartridges are missing," Mrs. Clement said slowly. Mrs. Law was silent as her face turned even paler than before.

The other children rushed up the steps. "We couldn't find a trace of him," said Charlotte.

Mrs. Law groaned weakly and crumpled onto the stoop, holding her head in her hands. "I know my son," she cried out. "He's gone to get the men who killed his father and brother. My son, my son..."

Laura stared at Mrs. Law and then at the Clements. Could such a young boy really have gone to the battlefield? Surely his mother's grief had turned her head.

Mr. Clement broke the silence. "You may be right. There's

no other reason for my musket disappearin'. It was there this mornin'."

Mrs. Law looked very determined. "I'll bring him back if I have to drag him with my own two hands. I'll not lose all my family on the same day."

"We'll go together," Laura said. "I want to go home to see if there is any news of James. May I leave the children here, Mrs. Clement? Fan and Bob and Charlotte will care for the younger ones. My baby takes milk from a cup now."

"Certainly they cin stay here. I wouldn't want the young-uns goin' back to Queenston, though I don't rightly think you should be goin' back there yourself, Laura."

"I'll be fine."

"What good cin you do? Better to stay away." Then she looked at Mrs. Law. "Still, May here could use the company... but, like as not, dear, you'll find John halfway there, shootin' at a rabbit."

"No, I won't. I know my son."

SIXTEEN

A strange stillness had settled over the town of Queenston. The streets were deserted and the pungent smell of sulphur hung thick in the damp air.

The women tramped down the empty street toward Laura's home at the foot of the Heights. As they reached the Secord yard, they heard the gunfire start again and, before Laura could stop her, Mrs. Law rushed toward the Heights.

"John...John!" she was screaming.

A musketball tore through her petticoat and grazed her leg. She fell instantly to the ground. Then, with blood soaking through her stocking from just above her ankle, she struggled to her feet. Unsteadily, she limped in and out among the men as she asked, "Have you seen a young boy?"

Laura stood still at the edge of her own dooryard, unable to do anything to help. Then a bareheaded soldier came limping toward Laura. She recognized him at once. It was Josh's young brother Elijah. Laura grabbed him just before he fell against her. With her support, he reached the house.

Inside, he slumped onto the couch in the hallway. "It's just my leg," he said. "There's others worse off."

"Have you seen James?"

"Not since early this morning. He was leading his men into the fighting."

"If you're all right, I'm going to look for my friend and her young son," Laura said. He nodded.

She rushed back to the edge of the lawn. Then she saw them. Mrs. Law was dragging her son, who was screaming and kicking at her. She walked with a bad limp, and her stocking was soaked in blood. Laura ran to them and took one of John's hands. With their combined effort, they pulled the hysterical boy into the house.

Inside, Laura poured water into a bowl to bathe the wounds. John had stopped fighting his mother now and was standing beside her, looking down with surprise at the blood on her torn petticoat and leg.

Laura worked rapidly, propping the woman's leg onto a kitchen bench, and the bleeding started to ease. "It's good it bled like that," Laura said. "It cleans the wound."

Mrs. Law showed no evidence of the pain she was enduring. Her thoughts were only for her son. "Don't let John get out again," she begged. "I'm afraid the boy's gone a bit daft."

"I'll talk to him," Laura promised. She had been watching him out of the corner of her eye as she worked on his mother's wound. He was sitting quietly on a footstool by the kitchen window, staring straight ahead.

Laura approached the boy and stood beside him for a moment before she spoke. He looked up at her sullenly. "Your mother is going to need your help to get back to the Clements' farm, John," Laura said in a quiet but firm voice. He looked at her again and said nothing. Laura waited.

"I've used up all my ammunition, anyway," John answered finally, "but I got some of 'em."

Laura turned away and walked to the bake table to tear strips of linen to bind Elijah's wound. He was wincing with pain now. She could hear John talking to his mother in the background.

"I hope your leg doesn't hurt too much to walk, Mother. I figure I should be taking back Mr. Clement's musket. I wouldn't want him to think I stole it. I figure I can work to pay him back for the cartridges."

"Don't worry 'bout it, son. I'll pay for them. We'd best be going now, but I'm going to need you to hang onto."

Before Laura could tend to Elijah again, she heard the door opening, and in stumbled half a dozen red-coated Queenston men.

"We've pushed them back up the Heights, but they've still

got possession of the top," said Joe Pine, one of the Lincoln militia.

"They're on the defensive. They're not attacking Queenston anymore."

"The Yanks are in control of the Heights and down around the cannon, but it's not working. Our men took care of that."

"Are you going back to attack?" Laura asked.

"Not now. We'll hold Queenston if they attack us, but we're waiting for Major General Sheaffe to come up from Fort George, and the Mohawks from Chippawa."

"Have many men been killed?"

"I don't know. But General Brock...General Brock..."

"I know."

"And Macdonell fell, too, but he's still breathing."

"The doctor says he'll not make it," said Joe.

"Have you seen James?" she asked.

The men hesitated then, and Joe looked down. She realized that he knew about her husband. "Please, tell me," she said.

"He's alive, but he's wounded and behind enemy lines. He fell just left of the cannon."

"How long before Sheaffe's men are expected?"

"Two or three hours, at least."

"...and James will be lying helplessly in the middle of a battle!"

"I'm afraid so, Laura."

Laura looked down then and spoke quietly to the men. She knew what she must do. "Help yourselves to anything in the kitchen—bread, cheese, milk," she said. They did not need urging, for they needed to keep up their strength. As they went into the kitchen, Laura slipped unnoticed out the back door.

At the foot of the Heights, she broke her run and walked briskly to the left, in the direction of the cannon.

"Where are you going, Laura? The enemy have control of the Heights," called a local volunteer soldier who was standing guard.

"I know. They also have my husband. He's wounded. I'm going for him." The soldier looked for help, but not a man stepped forward to stop her.

Her ankle-length white petticoat stood out starkly among the soldiers' dull uniforms. Her hair was tucked under her white cap.

Enemy soldiers saw the white figure approaching and alerted others. White was the symbol of parley and sometimes surrender between fighting soldiers. They watched with anticipation until they discerned that the approaching figure was only a slender young woman. What had she come for?

Oh, dear God, please help me, Laura breathed as she kept on advancing toward the enemy line.

Laura hesitated. The enemy was stationed just beyond.

Dead and wounded soldiers lay before her. She trembled as she heard their groaning. As she ran fearfully from one to the next to find her husband, she forgot that the enemy soldiers were watching her intently.

Suddenly, she saw James. He was lying very still on the ground between two standing American soldiers. One soldier had raised the butt of his gun in the air ready to strike.

"No!" Laura shouted.

The soldier looked up.

She ran and threw herself over James's body and screamed, "Kill me, not my husband!"

"Why not kill both of you?" the soldier snarled as he grabbed her arm and pulled her to her feet.

"She's too pretty to kill," the other soldier yelled, and yanked her over beside him.

Laura gasped for breath as she struggled to free herself.

"Stop!" A sharp command rang out.

Laura looked into the face of an American officer who had come up beside her.

"I apologize, Ma'am, for the conduct of my men," he said politely. Then he turned aside and barked, "Page and Johnson, take these two under guard."

Two more soldiers stepped forward from the other side of the battle site. They grabbed the weapons of the soldiers who had threatened Laura, then walked the offenders on up the

Heights, where they disappeared among the trees.

"You may take your husband home," the captain told Laura.

"Thank you," Laura said, with tears falling down her cheeks. Already she was beside James, holding his head in her hands.

"Please, James, try to sit up. Then you can lean on me."

He did not move.

"Here! Adams...Durham," the captain commanded. "Help this man to his home."

Another pair of soldiers stepped forward, tied their coats together, and lifted James onto the makeshift stretcher. They started slowly down the hill. James's arms hung down, limp.

Laura turned to the American captain who had helped. "Thank you. Thank you, Mr..."

"Captain Wool."

"Thank you, Captain Wool."

Then she ran to the men who were carrying James and directed them toward the Canadian line.

She walked in front and to one side so that the Canadian soldiers would see her first and allow the Americans to pass. When they reached the place where the Queenston men were guarding the ground they had gained, James roused himself a little and groaned. Then he slipped into unconsciousness again.

"We'd better take him directly to bed and not change coats here," the one soldier said.

The Queenston guards understood the situation and did

not object. "I'll go with you to make sure that you get back safely after you leave James," one of them volunteered.

They reached the house and carried James to a bed in the girls' room. Laura did not dare lead them to the other bedroom and the body of General Brock.

She thanked them at the door. They nodded and were gone. The soldiers standing in her kitchen watched in amazement.

"Please, go for the doctor," she said, putting a kettle of water on to boil. A soldier nodded and left by the back door.

She went back upstairs to James, who was groaning weakly. She could see two wounds, one in his leg and the other in his shoulder. She went to the girls' nightstand to get a jug of water. When she came back to the bed, James, delirious with fever, was calling her name.

"I'm here, James," she said, placing a cool cloth on his forehead.

Finally, she heard noise below and heavy steps. She walked out of the bedroom to see the doctor and another soldier at the foot of the stairs.

"Dr. Greenfield, thank God you've come," she cried out. The doctor started up the stairs to see James. Laura stared in disbelief at his clothes. He was splattered with blood and pieces of flesh. Even his face and hands were dirty with mud, blood, and grime. The stench from his clothes was worse than the smell of James's fresh wounds.

Up in the room, Laura quickly poured water from her pitcher into the china basin and handed the doctor a bar of her own strong lye soap.

He hesitated at first and then proceeded to wash his hands. He would please the lady, he decided. He had no energy left to quarrel with her.

She watched anxiously while the doctor examined James. He was conscious now and groaned feebly as the doctor probed his wounds. Finally, the doctor said, "I've got the ball from his shoulder, but I can't get the one in his knee."

Laura was relieved when James lapsed back into unconsciousness. For a few minutes, he was free from the pain and could not hear the doctor's comments. Dr. Greenfield finished dressing the wounds and walked out into the hall with Laura. "He will get better, won't he?" Laura asked.

"I can't say. Only God knows that, Laura. I'll venture to say, though, that if he lives through the night, he may make it. However, we'll have to amputate the leg if infection sets in, and with the bullet still there, it's bound to."

A feeling of powerlessness overcame Laura, and she grabbed the railing of the staircase to steady herself.

"These powders may help a little to keep the pain down. I'm sorry I can't leave more," the doctor said. "I must go now. There's to be another battle soon. I have to be ready for the injured."

Back in the kitchen, the kettle was boiling over, and

all the soldiers had gone except for the wounded Elijah. Dr.
Greenfield took a look at his wound and said he was in no
danger, but he'd be useless in the battle. Then the doctor left
for the emergency tent set up for the injured not far from the
battlefield.

"Where have the soldiers gone?" Laura asked Josh's
younger brother.

"To take the Heights," he said weakly. "Sheaffe's arrived,
and they've gone to line up with his men."

As Laura hastened back up the stairs and into the bedroom,
the thunder of cannon and spatter of heavy musket fire filled
the house. "Thank you, God, that James is not out there in
the middle of it," she mumbled aloud. At least there was that
relief. But turning toward James, who was moaning now and
moving his head back and forth on the pillow, she wondered if
there was any reason to hope.

Laura emptied the dirty water into the pail and poured
fresh, cool water into the china washbowl. She squeezed her
damp cloth and laid it across her husband's forehead. Already
she had cut away his dirty, blood-soaked uniform and removed
it from his body. She laid fresh, dry towels under his arms and
legs and sides. Then, with a clean cloth, she dipped into the
water and continued to bathe her husband's burning body as
he slipped in and out of consciousness.

James shifted restlessly in the bed and flailed his arms

about as he continued to mumble meaningless sounds—and his temperature kept rising. Only when he finally lay still did she notice how quiet it was outside. She rushed to the open window and listened intently. There was no gunfire.

Was it over? She could hardly believe that. Even if the shooting had stopped, it did not necessarily mean that she and James were out of danger. It was quite possible that Queenston had been taken by the enemy, and that American soldiers were already on their way to take possession of all the houses in town.

The body of General Brock lay in the other bedroom—if American soldiers came to take over the house, there would be no way of hiding the body from them. And she had heard that they did not always treat bodies of leaders with respect. Then she remembered that they would not recognize him, since his uniform had been changed.

She turned back to the danger at hand. She would have no way of defending herself and her husband from a band of celebrating soldiers. Only God could protect them now. Otherwise, they were completely at the mercy of the enemy.

She looked down at James again. For now, he was her greatest concern. His pain was as bad as ever. Glancing at the washstand, she noticed that the water was low in the pitcher. She took it up and ran downstairs for more water. She went by the clock in the hall. It was five o'clock in the afternoon. It seemed much later.

Out at the well beside the house, she rolled down the bucket and looked up toward the Heights as she worked. Near the bottom of the slope, not far from the edge of the yard, she could see men coming toward her. They were Queenston men. She recognized their dull red coats.

"We've gained the Heights," they shouted as they came nearer. "We've held it for two hours now. It's ours!"

"We've taken more than nine hundred American prisoners. They'll be marching them through the town."

Laura saw the blue-coated captives not far behind. Even the ones with blood-soaked wounds were forced to limp along. She stood riveted to the spot, looking at the haggard faces of the defeated soldiers. Suddenly, she was aware of the suffering of the enemy. Then she saw a familiar face. It was Captain Wool. Blood trickled from a shallow wound on the side of his face and his eyes looked glassy. The soldiers had stopped the prisoners to assemble them into lines, Captain Wool in front.

Laura grabbed her pail of water and the big dipper that hung on a nail by the side of the well and ran to the side of the road. She handed the dipper of water to Captain Wool, who gulped the water down, then handed the dipper back to her. As the soldiers refilled the dipper from the pail and drank, the pain in their faces lightened a little.

Captain Wool had not realized who she was. Then, as he

looked up to say, "Thank you," a glimmer of recognition crossed his face.

A Queenston soldier handed her the empty pail and she turned to refill it, but by the time it was full, the men had started marching down the road again.

Laura raced back to the house, where Elijah was still lying on the couch in the hallway. "We've won," she said, handing him a cup of water. He sighed and smiled.

At that moment, Laura heard someone at the door. Before she could rush to open it, James's brother, David, came in. "We've taken the Heights, Laura," he said. "Where's James? They told me you got him."

Laura led him up the stairs to the girls' room where James lay. James did not recognize his wife or his brother.

"The fever is high," she said. "I'm trying to keep it down with the cold water."

"Be careful, Laura. You don't want him going into pneumonia."

Laura remembered General Brock's body in their other bedroom. "David," she asked, "will they be coming for General Brock now?"

"I thought you knew," he said, surprised. "They came for his body early this morning. He was here very briefly. They took him to a safer house, farther from the American line."

"I didn't know," she said. "We could have taken James to

his own room. Still, he was better on this side of the house, farther from the noise of the battle. He needs stronger medicine, David. Will you try to find the doctor and get something more?"

"I'll try, but he's very busy. Goodbye, Laura." He turned then and hurried down the stairs and out the door.

Laura shook a little as she went back in the bedroom. Her hands trembled as she squeezed the excess moisture from her cloth and bathed her husband's brow. His eyelids opened, but he looked beyond her. His deep blue eyes were clouded and heavily bloodshot.

"Laura, Laura," he whispered, still not looking at her.

"I'm here, James."

He moved his hand and she took it. His strengthening grip told her he realized she was caring for him.

"Who's...winning?" He could barely say the words.

"We won, James. We've taken the Heights. It's a definite victory."

He relaxed his hold and slipped back into semi-consciousness. This time, he seemed more peaceful, and Laura felt he was resting.

Long past dark, Laura was still sitting at his bedside in the light of the flickering candles. Hearing footsteps on the stairs, she went out into the hallway and saw David Secord coming up the steps. His face was lined and smudged with dirt. Obviously he had not rested since the battle. Laura looked at him expectantly, hoping that he had brought more medication.

"How is he?"

"A little better, I think. He's resting more comfortably, and he recognized me a short time ago, but he still feels very hot. And he's in a lot of pain."

David looked down at his younger brother. "The doctor's too busy to come now," he sighed, "and he's run short of supplies, but we're expecting more from the fort."

"Is it really over?" she asked, looking for reassurance, though she herself had seen the enemy prisoners led through the town.

"Yes, for now."

"Was it a long battle on the Heights?"

"Not at the last. We had them surrounded and pushed them to the edge. Then Sheaffe gave the order that if they surrendered, their lives would be spared."

"What happened then?"

"They couldn't hear him in all the confusion. They were jumping off the cliff to their deaths to avoid the British bayonets or the Indian scalping knives."

"But those prisoners who went by..."

"Yes, we took some prisoners. I ran into their lines and shouted Sheaffe's promise. Then they listened."

"How did they know they could trust you?"

"My wife's father and brother were among them, and they reassured the others. They were just ready to jump, too, when they saw me and stopped."

"Thank God! But how brutal war is when men must fight their own kin! Were many of our men killed?"

"Fourteen, we think—far fewer than we expected—but two of those were Brock and Macdonell. The price for the Heights was high. There never has been a general like Brock and never will be again."

"I know. James loved him, too, as we all did."

"There's great mourning now, and it will spread all across Canada this week as the news gets out. He gave his life to hold the line till reinforcements came. If he had waited, they'd have taken Queenston." Then, breaking off abruptly, he turned toward the stairs again. "I must go now. Come down with me so you can latch the door."

"Why?"

"We think we have them all, but a few American deserters may be roaming about."

"Oh, I didn't realize we were still in danger," she said, following her brother-in-law.

"I wish I could stay to help."

"We'll manage. Your men need you." Laura knew that David Secord was a major.

"Good night, Laura."

"Good night."

Laura dropped the latch across the door and turned back into the kitchen. She picked up clean cloths and a kettle of hot water, and hurried back up the stairs to her husband. She knew it would be a long night.

SEVENTEEN

When the autumn sun rose on the morning of October 14, Laura was still sitting beside her husband's bed. Tired beyond measure, she had attended him all night as the wounds in his knee and shoulder became more and more inflamed. Not long after sunrise, James came fully awake for the first time since Laura had rescued him. Drops of perspiration fell from his forehead as he wrestled with his pain. Laura almost wished that he would slip back into unconsciousness. Finally, he fell into a fitful sleep.

Laura sat by the bedside. She had not slept since the day before yesterday. As she leaned over onto the bed, exhausted, she prayed for strength and for James. The doctor's grim prediction was still in her mind.

If there were more battles, James would not be going, she thought with some satisfaction. Then she wondered what James would think about that. He had so wanted to defend his land. Unlike so many of the settlers, he had not been indifferent to the American attack. He was convinced that the invaders had to be defeated. How would he feel if he could not continue as sergeant of his militia regiment?

* * *

Laura awakened to the sound of James calling her name. She did not know how long she had been sleeping. As she raised her head, she saw that he was tossing with fever again and moaning in pain.

She ran down to the kitchen, selected some herbs and ground them together in a wooden cup. Hooking a kettle over the fire, she waited for what seemed like hours before it boiled. The tea would soothe the pain, even if it didn't take it away.

Back in the girls' room, she held some of the tea to James's lips and put cold compresses on his wounds to cool the inflammation. His knee now looked worse than his shoulder.

The fever was rising again. Laura poured more water into the jug. Using linen cloths, she continued to bathe his body. She managed to comb out some of his blood-caked hair. Then his increasing groans told her she would have to stop, and he lapsed back into sleep.

Laura stood up to stretch, still keeping her eyes on her husband. She remembered again the doctor's warning about James's leg. Oh, dear God, please don't let it happen. Please, don't let James lose his leg. The thought of it made her feel sick in the stomach. Would they have to come in and hold him down while the doctor sawed off his leg above the knee? She almost fainted at the picture that flashed before her eyes.

She turned and held the back of her chair to get control of herself again, but the room seemed to be going black. She sat down and rested her head on her arms.

The feeling finally passed, and she got up to go downstairs to prepare food for herself and James. As she reached the foot of the stairs, she heard someone at the back door. She rushed out of kitchen into the hall and lifted the latch.

Her brother, Charles, stood there in his uniform. She reached up and wrapped both arms around him. "Charles, you're safe. Are you all right?"

"Yes, I'm fine," he answered almost lightly.

"I guess you weren't in the battles yesterday."

"I was in the second one, on the Heights. My first battle, Laura."

"Charles, how awful for you."

"I thought it would be, but it wasn't. I was with Major Thomas Merritt's Niagara Light Dragoons. His son, William Hamilton Merritt, and I were together through it all. I can tell you, we were dreading it after the events of the morning. We were too late for the first battle. We had come galloping into Queenston from Fort George only to find out the terrible news that Brock had fallen and the Yanks had taken the Heights. We were told to wait for Major General Sheaffe."

"The waiting must have been hard."

"I'll admit, Laura, I was fearful. We all were. It was as though the impossible had just happened. We thought that about two-thirds of the Canadian and British forces would be cut down, even if we did win the battle. Sheaffe led our troops the long way around from Fort George and out through the country. Then we crossed back again to attack from the west. It was the most tense ride of my life."

"Did you attack from the west?"

"The infantry, the 41st Regiment, and the local militia went up the Heights from the west, along with a battery of guns drawn by farm horses. We rode on the right flank."

"Expecting the worst?"

"Yes, but it was all over in ten minutes. We lost only fourteen men, and we'd expected to be slaughtered. We could hardly believe it when they surrendered. It was all over so fast, and we were still alive."

"Thank God."

"Well—the Mohawks on the right flank were ahead of us, along with Captain Runchey's Company of black soldiers. Those two companies surprised the Americans from the southwest and kept interrupting them with skirmishes while they were trying to build fortifications. So, by the time we got there, the enemy was vulnerable to our attack. Thank God for the Mohawks and the black soldiers!"

"I only hope the Americans stay home now."

"I doubt they will, but we've driven them out for now, and probably for the winter. Their casualties were high. We took over nine hundred prisoners, and they had over two hundred and fifty dead and several wounded. How is James?"

"Come and see. I can't leave him for long."

Charles followed her up the stairs.

James's eyes were open now, and he brightened a bit at the sight of Charles in uniform. James mumbled, "Are we holding the Heights?"

"We sure are. I doubt they'll ever try that again."

"But...General Brock..."

"I know," said Charles.

James grimaced with the pain, though he tried not to show it, and Laura nodded to Charles as she held the door. "I'll be right back, James," said Laura, going out behind Charles.

She followed Charles down the stairs. "Please try to get the doctor to come and see James again or at least get some pain medicine. He had so little before."

"I'll try."

Laura prepared more herbal tea, then returned to her husband. She kept on bathing him and, as night approached, she cleaned his wounds again.

When she was finished, James looked up at her and said in a whisper, "Laura, try to rest. I'll call if I need you."

She looked across at Harriet's bed.

"Go ahead, Laura."

Fully dressed, she crawled onto the bed and did not even stretch out before her eyes closed. James's face convulsed with pain, but he breathed deeply and did not cry out as he looked at his wife asleep across the room.

* * *

The sound of cannon going off nearby shook the air. "It's the gun salute...for General Brock," James murmured to Laura. Then they heard a salute from across the river.

"That sound came from Lewiston," said Laura. "Even his enemy salutes General Brock."

"He would have ordered the same for an enemy general."

Laura did not answer. Instead she said, "I'll go for more fresh water to clean your wounds, James."

"Laura, the pain has eased a little now. Can't we just leave them alone?"

"I suppose, but I'll need water anyway to be ready for later."

Laura left him then. She knew he was thinking about the funeral and the other wounded men in his company who would be absent, too.

The doctor finally called and said that James was out of

immediate danger. He gave her special instructions for the knee wound.

As Laura went out the back door, heading for the well, a brisk wind blew the leaves along the ground. The wind had blown away the leaves and left the trees looking bleak and lonely in the cold morning. Perhaps even the Heights mourned General Brock.

Still, Upper Canada had remained under British control, and James was alive. She bowed her head for a moment and whispered thanks.

Laura knew that most people were thinking the war would soon be over. No one had really wanted it in the first place, since many, like her, had close friends and relatives across the line. It was a political war that had been forced on the Americans and their government by the war hawks. Surely the American forces had been beaten so decisively at Queenston Heights that they would be called home. It would all be over before Christmas. She was thankful that neither she nor Mira had sons old enough to go to war. And Josh was so busy on his farm, she doubted he would ever be called into active duty, though she knew he had been called upon to train in a reserve force in case the States was invaded.

As she pulled her bucket up over the low stone wall around the opening of the well, she heard children's voices. Charlotte came running around the corner of the house and Harriet followed. Bob and Fan were behind with Charles.

Laura put down her bucket and held out her arms, a wide smile spreading across her face. She hardly remembered what it felt like to smile. Charles threw his arms around her neck.

"Mama, mama," he cried as he hugged her.

"We heard Papa was wounded," Charlotte said. "How serious is it?"

"He's improving. He's still very weak but not as feverish."

"They made us bring them back, Ma'am," said Fan. "They just wouldn't believe your brother Charles. He told us you and Mister James was all right."

"I'm so glad to be home." Harriet twirled around with joy. "I'm glad this war is over. We thought it would never end!"

"Yes, dear, it's over—but you all need to be very quiet, for your father was badly wounded. He's in your room and too weak to go back to his own yet. You girls may sleep in our room. Charlotte, you can watch Charles in the cradle. I must stay near your father; he still needs me. Now, come quietly and you may see him, but only for a minute."

EIGHTEEN

It's a bloody disgrace," said James. "Sheaffe should have stood his ground and fought, instead of destroying his own ship and running with his troops."

Spring had finally come and with it the unexpected news that York had been invaded and captured. A Canadian frigate, the *Isaac Brock*, had been burned in the harbour by order of Major General Sheaffe before he withdrew his men. Within a day, the Americans had taken over. Now James was sitting in the armchair beside the kitchen window, fuming over what he felt was an act of great cowardice.

"Thank God for Strachan up there at York. If he hadn't taken over and negotiated with the enemy, it would have been even worse. Imagine an Anglican priest having to take charge instead of the military."

"The poor people," Laura said as she thought of the looting.

"The Reverend Doctor blames the plundering on our own

leader, Sheaffe. When the fleeing British army blew up the York magazine, a huge boulder killed several Americans and their leader, General Pike, just as he was moving in to take York. The American soldiers were furious at the loss and spent their anger against the people and property of York."

"Please don't concern yourself with it, James. Nothing can be done now."

"Strachan's right, Laura. He's right. The country will be ruined by Sheaffe's defensive warfare. We need another Brock with the courage to lead his men. His offensive tactics worked. Sheaffe will not only bring us defeat, he'll make us a laughing-stock while he's at it."

Laura was not sure who was right, but she was certain that James's irritation wasn't doing him any good. His shoulder wound had healed, but he was still unable to put his full weight on the leg with the wounded knee. Even after the long winter, it had not healed. In fact, just lately, the wound seemed to have become more infected. James had spent most of his time in their room with his leg stretched out on a fat feather pillow. The throbbing pain was unbearable when he stood.

Laura helped James back up to his room and had just re-turned to the kitchen when she heard a heavy pounding on the front door. She set down the bread pans she was bringing out and reached for a cloth to wipe her hands. Who would be passing by so early in the morning?

She pulled open the door and stood in surprise as three grey-coated American soldiers stared at her. Word had come to Queenston that the American forces were moving around the western tip of Lake Ontario to Burlington Bay and toward Newark, but she had not expected to see enemy soldiers at Queenston. Perhaps these were advance scouts.

"May we have water and food, Missus?" one of the soldiers asked politely.

She noticed how boyish they looked. They reminded Laura of her brother Charles. "Yes," she replied.

They were armed so she had to do as they said. She prayed that James would not call out for her. They might become alarmed if they heard a man's voice and shoot her husband before they realized how weak he was. And if she volunteered to tell them about him, would they believe her or would they think it was a trick?

They followed her directly into the kitchen. Laura was surprised to see them take their shakos from their heads and put them on the hall table as they passed through. Then the three young soldiers sat down quietly on the bench beside the kitchen table as she laid out dishes for their meal. She noticed that they were looking around the room with admiration. One nudged the other and pointed to her glassed-in cabinet in the corner. Most of the good dishes displayed there had come from Great Barrington and had belonged to her mother before her.

She took in a deep breath and watched them as her anger grew. Yet she said nothing.

"I must go out to the cellar to get meat," she said quietly. She hoped they would not follow to see where she kept their food supply, so she added, "You might like to sit in the parlour while you wait."

They nodded and followed her as she led them into her best room. They smiled with satisfaction, and two of them slumped down on the sofa while the third sat in the large chair nearer the warmth of the fireplace. As he leaned back in comfort, he stretched out his long legs until they nearly reached the hearth.

"Reminds me of home," he said to the other two.

Seeing them quietly settled, Laura ran out the back door to Bob and Fan, who were working at the large oven in the bakehouse. She told them about the soldiers and gave instructions for the meal.

Laura saw Charlotte and her other children returning from the store. "Go back to our store," she said, after explaining what had happened.

"Shall I take Charles with us?" Charlotte asked.

"No, he'll be fine with me. You run along now. Go to the other side of the shed and don't pass where they can see you from the parlour window." Charlotte was now a beautiful girl of fifteen with curly dark hair. She looked very much like her cousin Phoebe.

Laura took the fresh coffee pot from the hearth, put it on a tray with three cups, and took the tray in to the men in the front room.

"Your meal will be ready soon," she told them.

"Thank you, Missus," they said.

"You'd think I'd invited them to dinner," Laura grumbled to herself.

She shut the door behind her as she came out of the parlour, then silently went up the stairs and across to James's room. She held her finger to her lips, and James, alerted by her pale countenance, knew that all was not well. She quickly whispered into his ear and left.

She brought a fresh apron down from the linen cupboard in case the men had seen her and wondered why she had gone upstairs. To her relief, the door to the parlour was still closed. They had probably not noticed anything.

She had not been in her kitchen long when Bob and Fan came in with the steaming food. They had prepared fresh creamed potatoes and carrots, and pork fried in maple syrup. Some apple pies were baking now, to be ready by the time the Americans had finished their first course. Bob and Fan set the serving dishes on the table and went back out to the bakehouse.

Laura took out some of her best dishes. Perhaps if she

treated the soldiers well, they would leave her house without taking anything. She could not forget the stories she had heard of the plundering of York, even after a peace treaty was signed. The American officers had not been able to control their men, or had pretended they were not able.

The three young soldiers ate as though they hadn't had a good meal in weeks. When Fan came in with steaming apple pies, Laura added a large chunk of cheese to each plate.

"It's just like Ma's pie," the youngest one said when he ate his first bite. He smiled openly at Laura. "I'll be glad, Missus, when this is all over, and we can go back home."

"Not me," his older friend said. "When we come for good to this country, we'll divide the land, and I'll take this here for my share." He looked around the room and rested his eyes on Laura's built-in china cabinet.

Suddenly, unable to contain her outrage, Laura burst out, "You scoundrel, all you'll ever get here will be six feet of earth."

They were silent after that. She was no longer the hostess, and they her guests. They were the enemy. The soldiers looked at Laura suspiciously as they finished their last few mouthfuls of pie and left without losing any time.

As Laura watched them go, she regretted her outburst.

"I was wrong to be so vindictive," she said to James when she had gone back upstairs. "They were mostly polite and took nothing from me except food, which I would gladly give to any hungry strangers. I had no right to speak to them the way I did, even if they were enemy scouts." Laura was not sure that they really were scouts, and she could not leave James to find out.

She heard soon enough. A few days later, on May 27, 1813, the Americans attacked and took Newark. The soldiers must have been advance scouts. Her brother Charles had been at Newark with the Provincial Dragoons, trying to defend the town. It had been a bloody battle, with heavy losses on both sides. The British had been outnumbered four to one.

Two days after news of the battle reached her, Laura had gone to St. David's to see if Charles's fiancée, Elizabeth, or her mother, Hannah, had received any word from Charles. She was surprised to find Charles there himself. He had been injured and was resting in one of the bedrooms upstairs. He described the slaughter to Laura. "In one plot of land no wider than fifteen feet and no longer than two hundred yards, there were at least four hundred wounded and dead men. If my friend William had not seen me lying there and dragged me to safety and taken me on the back of his horse, I'd have died."

"Rest now, Charles," Laura had said.

Glassy-eyed with fever, Charles insisted on continuing. "Brigadier-General Vincent—"

"Who's he?"

"The commander of the Centre Division. He ordered us out. He said the fort was lost. He ordered the magazine blown up and started us on the road to Queenston. Then he directed us across by St. David's. William brought me right here to the Secords. I'd never have made it on my own."

Elizabeth walked into the room with a bowl of water and clean towels.

"I know you'll take good care of him," Laura said to Charles's frail fiancée, who looked almost as pale as Charles.

"He'll be fine," Elizabeth said, for Charles's sake, as she tried to smile.

* * *

Although the doctor had not been able to take the bullet out of her husband's knee, his salves had been helping the wound lately, and James had been able to sit for a short time each day. Laura hurried home because he would be ready to get up. She wanted to tell him the news about Newark before someone else did. She hoped it would not set him back again.

When she came to her backyard, Laura noticed two horses tied by the fence. She hurried toward her house, wondering who had come for a meal this time.

From the hallway, Laura could hear the voice of the young enemy soldier who had liked her apple pie.

"So, they've come back to claim this here property," she thought.

As she passed through the hall, Laura saw two shakos on the

hall table. In the kitchen, Fan rushed around preparing food.

As Laura approached the soldiers, she controlled her feelings and greeted them as if they had just come by on a visit. "So, you've come back for more of that pie like your ma's," she said to the younger one.

He smiled and said a bit bashfully, "Thank you, Missus. We'd like that." They were sitting on the bench beside the table.

"And where's your other friend? There were three of you last time."

The young soldier looked down. "You were right about the six feet of earth, Missus."

The third man had been killed at Newark.

NINETEEN

I've come for some of your baking, Missus," the old woman spoke in a squeaky voice that did not seem quite real.

Laura stared at the large, bent figure standing at her kitchen door. A close-knit woollen shawl covered her head and crossed over her short gown. The front of a beribboned mob cap poked out over her forehead. Her heavy petticoat hung well over her shoes as she waited on the back stoop, holding her empty round basket.

Laura did not hesitate to welcome the old woman, for she had never forgotten her outburst against the three young American soldiers. Now she kept food prepared and ready to serve to anyone who passed her way. Most often it was the enemy. Praise for Laura Secord's apple pie and candied maple sugar spread through the lines as more and more American soldiers received her hospitality. So Laura was not surprised to see this woman at her door.

"What would you like?" Laura said in a pleasant voice. The coarse-featured old lady shifted from one foot to the other. It was late at night, and Laura could see that she was tired. James and the children were already in bed, and the servants, Bob and Fan, had retired to their quarters.

"I'd pay for a bite to eat, Missus," the woman continued in a squeaky voice. The woman looked down and shifted uncomfortably again.

Laura looked sadly at the bent figure and said, "Come in, please. If you wish, you may rest in the kitchen while I prepare you a bite." The woman stepped forward and hurried inside.

She sat down heavily in the rocking chair by the window, and Laura began to warm potatoes and cook eggs in an iron frying pan over a low fire in the hearth. This war had made her unduly suspicious, she decided, for she couldn't help wondering about the old woman. Why was she far from home? They were at war.

When Laura turned from stirring her potatoes, the woman said, "Do you have extra butter? I supply butter regularly to the troops stationed out of town, and I have none left."

"And where is your home?" Laura asked.

"Eh?" the woman asked. She cupped one hand around her ear as she looked up at Laura.

"Your home? Where are you from?"

"Near Stoney Creek. Have you any butter for sale?"

"I'll get a few bowlfuls from the fruit cellar later. You are a long way from home."

Laura hurried about the room. Well, at least the woman had offered to pay. She sighed as she took a tin plate from the cupboard and placed it on the table. With a long wooden ladle, she pushed the hot potatoes and eggs onto the large plate. She was just about to tell the woman to sit at the table when she noticed her at the other side of the room, peering into the china cabinet.

"Your food is ready," Laura said a little crisply.

The woman turned around quickly then, but spoke in the same shaky voice. "You must have brought these dishes from the old country." She slid along the bench seat beside the table. Her long unfashionable petticoats dragged along the floor.

"No, they came from Great Barrington, Massachusetts," said Laura. "They were my mother's."

The woman suddenly choked on the huge mouthful she had just scooped up, and Laura rushed over to a pail on the bake table. She dipped out a cup of water and handed it to her.

"Here," she said. "This may help. You needn't hurry. Take your time eating." She was beginning to feel sorry for the woman.

Laura bent over the fireplace to cover the coals with ashes, for it was a warm day in late May, and she hoped the fire would not heat the rest of the house. In this position, squatting over the hearth, she glimpsed across at the woman, who was still clearing her throat. Beneath the table, her feet were spread wide apart and her boots were not a woman's.

She knew that sometimes women wore their husband's boots, but these boots were different; they were military boots. A British soldier would not try to hide his identity, and neither would an American soldier. A cold chill gripped her as she realized he must be a scavenger. He could well be more dangerous than the enemy, but she knew she must feed him anyway.

She stayed crouched there, poking the ashes and trying to compose herself. She would have to go along with his disguise for now. She needed to figure out a way to lure him outside, give him the butter, and then hurry back inside and lock the door. Maybe she would come to no harm. She slowly straightened up and turned toward the table.

His plate was empty.

"Let's go out for the butter now," she said quietly. But her hand shook a little as she picked up the plate from the table. She felt the eyes of the scavenger close upon her.

"Don't be afraid, Laura Ingersoll," said a low, smooth voice.

Laura turned and stared at the figure before her. She had not been called Laura Ingersoll for years now. Who was this person?

"I was Laura Ingersoll before I married. My husband is James Secord, a sergeant with the first Lincoln Militia."

"Laura…I'm Red," the man said in a strong masculine voice, pulling the heavy grey wig from his head and letting his shock of thick red hair fall over his forehead.

Laura stared in disbelief. The man's unruly hair was standing on end, just as it had when she had first met him, and his face, though fuller now, had broken into that lopsided smile she could never forget. It truly was Red.

"Red!" she shouted and rushed over to him, but hesitated and dropped her arms without throwing them around him.

Still smiling, he said in a low voice, "Be quiet, Laura. I'm on the run again." He grabbed the wig from the table and pulled it back over his head. "But tell me about yourself."

"First, I'll get you some of my apple pie," she said, cutting him a huge wedge.

"Thank you," he said. "Now, tell me."

"Well, we came to Upper Canada in 1795," said Laura, taking a chair by the window. "Father ran the tavern at Queenston at first. Then he set up farming out at La Tranche River."

Red was eating pie slowly as she talked. "He must be torn by this war," he said.

"Yes, he would have been. He had many friends in America, as well as Mira and her husband and family. But he died just as it began. He never knew."

"And Sally?"

"She's at Port Credit, running the inn there. They lost the

farm." She swallowed as she thought about her father. Then she looked up at Red and asked, "And you, Red, why didn't you ever write? I haunted the mailbox."

"I did. I wrote to the judge, and I wrote to you, too."

"There was no return address on your letter to the judge, and I never received any letters."

"I didn't write you at the same time as I wrote the judge. But I wrote you not long afterwards. My letter must have been lost. Then I wrote again a few years after that. I guess you'd moved to Canada by then. I never forgot you, Laura, but I gave up hope of ever seeing you again." His voice was deep with emotion as he stared at her, and his fork lay still beside his plate.

Red was a handsome man, she thought, probably a few years younger than James—more her age. He adjusted his wig with one hand, and his pale green eyes swept softly across her face. She had forgotten that she had removed her mob cap before he had come, and her shining brown hair hung down long across her back and shoulders. He silently admired her as she sat there by the window, with the evening shadows falling across her face.

They sat in silence for a few minutes as though the years had not passed between them. Finally, he stood and walked over to her. He took her hand in both of his and said simply, "Thank you again, Laura."

She looked up into his handsome face and remembered the

boy she had cared so much about and had waited and waited to hear from.

"Mama!" It was Charles, crying out in his sleep.

Laura came back to the present with a start and pulled her hand free. The child did not call out again. Then she looked back at Red, still standing there, and she wondered why Red was running again.

"And you, Red," she asked. "Where are you going?"

Then, in a lower voice, "I mean, who or what are you running from this time?" There was no sting in her tone.

"I'm sorry. I can't explain." He sounded embarrassed.

She knew he was hiding from someone, or he would not have been dressed as he was. Suddenly, her feelings changed and she said, "There was some excuse then, but now you're a man. What justifies your running now?"

His voice became guarded.

"You're right," he said. "And I must go. May I buy the butter?"

He grabbed his large basket and handed it to her. She knew he wanted it for a cover, as it was not unusual for peddlers to go through a camp of soldiers, selling their goods. This way, he would pass undetected.

"I'll fill it from the cold cellar." She walked briskly to the door.

In about five minutes, she was back. He was sitting on

the back stoop. She handed him the basket filled with wooden bowls of butter packed in ice chips and sawdust.

He put a handful of money in her hand, but she did not even look at it as she saw him go out the door. For some reason, he had irritated her. Perhaps it was his irresponsibility. It seemed he would never grow up.

Then her heart softened as she thought of the poor shivering boy back on the road to Great Barrington. "God go with you," she called out gently.

He turned then and smiled. "We'll meet again, Laura. I will come back to see you."

She smiled sadly at Red, limping like an old woman as he went along the road to St. David's. She was quite sure she would never see him again.

TWENTY

The sultry summer days grew longer and hotter as the war that was to have ended so quickly dragged on into its twelfth month. The Americans controlled a large part of the Niagara Peninsula. Sheaffe had been recalled to England, and Brigadier-General John Vincent, commander of Britain's Centre Division, had withdrawn to Burlington Heights and disbanded the local volunteers. With three thousand American soldiers to seven hundred Canadian, the outcome of the war appeared to be inevitable. In the northern part of the Niagara Peninsula, the only local men still fighting were the cavalry of Captain William Hamilton Merritt.

Only one leader, an Irishman named James FitzGibbon, still dared to inhabit the lower region of the Peninsula. He had been an officer under Brock and had learned from him and admired his war strategy. His small, well-trained band, known to the Americans as the "green sliver" and the Bloody Boys, made lightning-speed skirmishes against the enemy. They travelled from place to place, signalling each other with cow bells.

* * *

On the evening of June 21, 1813, Laura was helping James up the stairs to bed. That afternoon, the temperature had reached ninety-eight degrees, and it was so hot on the second floor that James had spent the afternoon lying on the sofa in the parlour. His wound was still inflamed and gave him a lot of pain when he tried to stand on it. Laura noticed his weight on her shoulder more than usual this night. The heat was taking its toll.

They had barely reached the top of the stairs when Laura heard loud knocking at the front door. Wearily, she realized it would probably be enemy soldiers looking for food. They must be newcomers—soldiers who had been here before came to the back door that led to the kitchen.

The knocking had become louder, and she could hear sounds of shouting and jeering. This was a rougher bunch than usual. But she could not lock them out. "Dear God, protect us," she prayed as she led James into their room, then raced back down the stairs.

With trembling hand, she opened the door and looked up at a tall man with a long face and a large nose. His piercing blue eyes stared at her coldly as he gave orders to his men.

"Search the place."

Laura spoke out firmly and pleasantly, "I'll be glad to show you about. My wounded husband has been given permission by American officers to stay home, and my young children have gone to bed for the night."

Their leader nodded to two of his men and indicated that they should come with him. They followed Laura up the stairs. Laura could hear the other men searching the yard and the rooms below.

When Laura and the men returned to the main floor, she opened the door to the parlour and said, "I'll prepare you a meal quickly while you wait in here, if you wish."

Their leader agreed and his men entered. He stayed in the hallway, looking out the window.

"I'm going to the bakehouse to call my servants to help," she explained as she went outside. He followed, not far behind, and when he saw only the two black servants, he returned to the back stoop.

Bob and Fan had already prepared most of the meal. Laura kept partially cooked food in her deep cellar so that the preparation would not take long. She was thankful that they had the fireplace and pit in the bakehouse. A fire inside tonight would have made the upstairs unbearable for sleeping.

In about twenty minutes, the meal was ready, and Laura brought the serving dishes into the kitchen. She set the table and called the rough men in from the parlour. They slid eagerly along the benches on either side of the table. Laura had opened both the front and the back windows and, just as they were ready to eat, a pleasant breeze blew through the room and across the table.

They didn't notice. They helped themselves to huge portions and started eating right away, not like most of the other soldiers, who had waited until they were served. Their total concentration on their eating had one advantage, though. It gave Laura a chance to tiptoe up the stairs to check on the family.

The girls were not yet asleep, and she tried to reassure them with a smile. Then she looked in on James. He motioned her over and, as she bent her head toward him, he whispered, "It's that bastard Chapin and his turncoat partisans." She nodded and stepped back out into the hall. She dared not stay longer, lest she arouse suspicion. Trembling, she held the stair railing for a few seconds before she returned to the kitchen.

Laura set her last three pies on the table in front of the leader. Without thanks, he grabbed one, helped himself to a large piece, and passed the rest on to his men, who had already eaten plenty. They hardly noticed her as they continued to eat and talk.

Laura went out the back door and sat on the stoop, where it was a little cooler. She could hear the conversation of the men inside coming out through the kitchen window.

"That green sliver is getting too bold, Doctor. The men

sure didn't expect to run into him at Deffield's Inn today," a voice said.

Laura knew that Chapin had been a surgeon in Fort Erie and later Buffalo before the war.

"I'd think the two of them could have beat him up, at least, even if they didn't capture him," Chapin replied.

"He took them by surprise, Doctor."

"Taking a man by surprise is his style, and I plan to do something about it."

"Do you think Boerstler will take your advice, sir?" asked another.

"Of course he will. He'd be a fool not to," Chapin bragged. "Now's our chance to get rid of that green sliver and his Bloody Boys. Boerstler will listen to me."

"So, Captain, we attack the day after tomorrow?"

"Yes, we'll combine forces with all Boerstler's troops at Fort George and march down on the last foothold in the Niagara Peninsula. When he's wiped out, Upper Canada is ours!"

"He's a tough one, though. It may not be easy."

"He doesn't have nearly as many men as we do. Besides, we'll take him by surprise."

Laura sat frozen to the stoop. What if they came out and saw her sitting there? Surely they must know she was nearby. Perhaps it did not matter. What good could hearing them do? She was behind enemy lines, and it would be impossible for her to take the news to FitzGibbon.

Laura walked quietly to the well and sat on the far side of the low stone wall around the well opening. From there she could hear voices and guffaws but could not distinguish words. The front door slammed. She had taken the bucket from the well and set it on the low foundation wall when she heard footsteps coming toward her.

Chapin and his men stood beside her. She gulped down her fear and handed Chapin the dipper. To her relief, all he did was take a drink and offer his men the same. Then the churlish crew went on their way. Laura breathed a prayer of thanks as she went back into the house and walked upstairs to see James. They had not ransacked her home, as had happened twice before, and had not harmed her family.

Laura could see the relief in James's face when she told him the guerrillas were gone. Before she could say a word about what she had overheard, Charles cried out in his sleep. The heat was making him restless. She went to the cradle and wiped Charles's face with a cool cloth, her mind racing. Lieutenant FitzGibbon should be warned. He must not be taken by surprise. As it was, he would be far outnumbered by Boerstler's troops. She needed to talk to James.

When Laura finally turned back to her husband, she knew his pain was bad tonight. His dark head lay still against the pillow. His face was pale and his eyes intense. As usual, he did not complain, but he was obviously in no condition to talk. She had to tell him, though, and she did, recounting all the details she had heard.

"We can't be sure there will even be an attack," James whispered. "Chapin is known to be a braggart. He has no real power. Boerstler may well not listen to his suggestion. You've probably," he grunted in pain, "only heard the ravings of a man impressed with his own importance."

"Still, I wish your brother David or someone else would happen along so I could tell them."

"That won't happen now. All our men have been evacuated. There's no point in their risking coming into enemy territory."

"I also heard Chapin and his men talking about a run-in two of their men had with FitzGibbon just today. It seems he beat them up at Deffield's Inn, single-handedly. As far as I could tell, Chapin has a personal grudge against FitzGibbon."

"Ah..." James frowned. "And if he does persuade Boerstler, all of Upper Canada is in danger. FitzGibbon and his men are the only soldiers left inland in the southern part of the Peninsula. They've set up now at the home of militia Captain John De Cew at Beaver Dams. The rumour is that De Haren's men to the north and Bishop's, stationed even farther north on the southern shore of Lake Ontario, are outnumbered by the enemy. If they take FitzGibbon, they've got the Peninsula— and they may soon have Upper Canada!"

"James, somebody ought to tell Lieutenant FitzGibbon they are coming."

"Well, if I crawled on my hands and knees, I could not get there in time."

"Well, suppose I go?"

"You go? With the country in so disturbed a state? I doubt a man could get through, let alone a woman."

"You forget, James, that God will take care of me."

James was silent then for some time.

Half an hour later, he was asleep, and Laura slipped out of the room. She went down to the kitchen to prepare for the next day's breakfast. She thought of her children and her husband as she set out their porridge bowls. She didn't really have a choice. She would carry her message to FitzGibbon.

TWENTY-ONE

In the darkness, Laura lay still against James's shoulder. When dawn came, she sat up quietly on the edge of the bed, but James woke up and reached out to her. Wondering how to tell him her decision, she turned and grasped his hand and squeezed it.

But he knew.

"God go with you, Laura," he whispered.

In a moment, she had pushed her feet into her shoes and slipped into an ankle-length petticoat and yellow-flowered short overgown. Before she left the room, she pulled the cradle nearer to the bed so her husband could rock the baby if he awakened.

Then Charles did wake up and cried in the darkness. She stopped and stroked his temples until she felt him relax into a quiet sleep again. She hoped it would be a cooler day.

Down in the kitchen, she hastily ate the bread and cheese

she had set out the evening before, not knowing when she would eat again. Taking a lunch would certainly arouse suspicion if she were stopped by a sentry.

As she slipped out into the darkness, she prepared herself to answer any guard or scout who might question her. Neighbours had reported seeing enemy scouts from Fort George in the area lately.

She hurried along toward the cowpath that led to St. David's, a route that was used less frequently than the main road. From St. David's, she would go through the Black Swamp. She knew she would not need to fear the patrols there, for they would not risk encountering the dangerous rattlesnakes and the quicksand in the swamp. She trembled at the thought. It would take long hours to get through the swamp and to walk the trail to Twelve Mile Creek. From there, she would still have to find her way to the lieutenant.

"Halt!" a man shouted as she jumped down from the rail fence onto the cow trail. "Where do you think you're going?"

She turned slowly to face him. In the half-light, she could not tell if he was one of Chapin's guerrillas or an enemy scout from Fort George. She did not hesitate to answer. "I'm going to visit my brother, Charles Ingersoll, wounded and sick at the home of Mrs. Stephen Secord, a widow in St. David's."

"Why are you leaving so early? The sun is just rising."

"It's cooler now. I could faint along the way if I waited

until the heat of the day. I've come this way because this path is cooler than the main road to St. David's."

The guard walked closer and scrutinized her carefully. He had no doubt that this pale, thin woman really did need to travel in the fresh morning air. He believed her story because he knew that her brother and other wounded men had been allowed to stay in St. David's. He nodded her on.

The light was increasing as she hurried ahead. She could see a farm woman with her dog, rounding up some cows for the morning milking.

The sun had risen by six a.m. when Laura reached her sister-in-law's home in St. David's. She rapped lightly on the back door. A startled Hannah Secord opened it to see Laura standing on her back stoop. Her surprise soon turned to alarm as she said, "Whatever is it, Laura? What is the matter? Is it James?"

"No. My family's well."

"Come in, come in. Now, what is it?" she asked as Laura sat down in the nearest chair. No one else was in the room, but still Laura put her finger to her lips to show the need for secrecy.

Instantly Hannah knew her message concerned the war. In these times, walls were sometimes too thin. In the Peninsula, where there was such a mixture of people, Loyalists and American settlers, one just couldn't be certain who was loyal to whom.

"May I see my brother?" Laura asked. "I have come before the heat gets too unbearable."

"By all means, Laura, but first come with me for a bite of breakfast." Inside the kitchen, Hannah closed the door and fastened the windows tightly.

Charles's fiancée, Elizabeth, stood by the table, setting the dishes for the morning meal. She turned in surprise when Laura came into the room. "Oh, Laura—have you come to see Charles? He is improving." She recovered herself. "It's slow, but he is a little better."

"I'm grateful for your care and devotion, Elizabeth."

Elizabeth blushed and turned away. She went to the cupboard for bread and butter to set before Laura.

"Now, Laura, you may speak," Hannah whispered.

Laura quickly explained about Chapin's plan of attack on FitzGibbon.

"My dear, you are attempting the impossible. The road from St. David's to Beaver Dams is regularly patrolled by enemy scouts. You would not be allowed to pass through. It's simply an impossible task."

"But I don't need to go by that road. I'll travel a little north across country from here to Shipman's Corners. That'll take me through the Great Black Swamp. No soldier will be looking for anyone there."

"What are you saying, Laura? You can't go through that

swamp. If you do avoid the quicksand, you may very well be bitten by a rattlesnake."

"I have to get this message to them. James can't go, and I can't think of anyone else who can. I feel certain that fate has let me hear this message. I must go. I can only trust that God will direct me through the swamp and beyond."

"Oh, Laura. I'm afraid for you."

"I'm going with you," Elizabeth volunteered. "If we come to quicksand, I can help. We'll walk apart, and if one of us is sucked in, the other will be able to help. That swamp is just too dangerous for anyone alone."

"It's too dangerous for anyone at all," Hannah mumbled. "You're too frail to attempt it, Elizabeth."

"May I go with you, Laura?" Elizabeth asked again.

"You and Hannah decide. But while you're thinking about it, can you take me up to see Charles, Elizabeth? I'd like to see him for a minute. Is he awake?"

As they went up the stairs, they knew he was awake, for they could hear a low groaning. The sound stopped when they entered the room.

Charles was sitting on the edge of the bed, but he slumped back on the pillows as they came over to him. Perspiration stood out on his face.

"Oh, Charles!" said Laura.

"It only hurts when I move, but I can't go on lying here

when my dragoons need me. I must be ready soon to return to the troops."

"The fever comes back when he moves around much," Elizabeth explained.

"I won't stay long, Charles. I just came to check on you before the day was too hot."

Laura squeezed her brother's hand. They did not talk long, for Charles was obviously in great pain, and Laura was able to excuse herself soon without arousing his suspicion. She did not want him to carry the burden of her mission. She left the room quickly, with Elizabeth close behind.

When they reached the lower hall, Elizabeth said, "I'm going with you as far as Shipman's Corners. I'll tell Mother."

Laura slowly started away from the house and down the lane alone, but Elizabeth caught up to her before she reached the road. There they turned and waved to Hannah, who stood in the doorway.

They scanned the horizon for any sign of an approaching horse or man. All was still as they reached the edge of the swamp. Laura tried to appear confident so the fear would leave Elizabeth's eyes. But she found that difficult as they entered the dense undergrowth.

Elizabeth tried to smile. "It's best we walk apart."

"Yes, in case of quicksand. I think we should each get a sturdy stick to feel ahead of us," Laura advised. She thought of another use for the sticks, but she didn't mention that—the sticks would help fight wild animals or snakes.

Armed with an old branch, Laura led the way through the thick brush and undergrowth. Neither of them spoke. They were using all their energy to push ahead. The branches caught and tore at their petticoats as they fought their way through. They kept swatting at the mosquitoes and horse flies that attacked them in swarms.

Suddenly, Laura felt one foot sinking. Slowly and steadily, she pulled back while she leaned on her other leg and her stick. She gradually drew her foot from the mud, but her shoe was gone. When Elizabeth came up close behind her and saw Laura's shoe was lost, she offered one of hers. "No, I can't take it," Laura said.

"I'm only going to Shipman's Corners. You have to last much longer. Take it," Elizabeth replied more forcefully.

Reluctantly, Laura accepted the shoe. It was too tight but it protected her foot well. They went on ahead. When they came to a thicket of thorny bushes, Elizabeth bravely kept from crying out as she stepped on a sharp stone.

Eventually the ground below them seemed less swampy. "I think it's not far now," Laura said. They could see a few huge rocks ahead, the ideal spot for a rattlesnake. They moved slowly, looking and listening for rattlers.

They had just passed the rocky outcropping when Elizabeth declared, "I'm sorry, I have to rest." She lowered herself to a small rock at the side of the path.

As Laura turned back to her, she saw that her foot was bleeding where she had cut it on the stone. "I'll not wear this any longer," Laura said. She put the shoe in Elizabeth's hand. The younger woman hesitated at first and then accepted it.

"We must continue on," encouraged Laura, "if I'm to reach De Cew's by tonight."

It was then that they heard the distinct sound of a rattler about to strike. They froze like statues.

Laura instinctively held her breath and waited.

Then they heard a slithering in the bushes, and Laura knew they had been saved from disaster. Shaken, but strengthened in her resolve to complete the mission, she turned to the terrified Elizabeth.

"I can't go farther...I can't..." Elizabeth said with a scarcely audible sob.

"We're almost there, Elizabeth. Look through the branches and trees. I can see clear sky...a blue patch...the end of the swamp."

"Well, there's no sound now," Elizabeth responded. "I guess it's better to go on."

After another arduous slog that was farther than it looked, they emerged into the light again and out of the dangers in the swamp.

The full heat of the windless late June day hit them, and their eyes stung. Elizabeth staggered at first as she adjusted to the light and the intensity of the heat. Laura put out her hand and steadied her. Sweating heavily, they reached the main road that led to Shipman's Corners. As the houses of the little settlement came into view, Laura said, "I'm going south now."

"No, Laura. Come with me," Elizabeth pleaded. "It's too far and too dangerous. You'll never make it."

"No, Elizabeth, I'm going on," Laura replied.

Elizabeth stooped and took off her shoe. "You must take this," she said. "I'm almost there."

Laura smiled at her friend, took the shoe, and headed down the road to the south.

TWENTY-TWO

Twelve Mile Creek didn't usually flow fast in the month of June, but the spring rains had turned it into a torrent of rough waves that swirled out toward the banks and jackknifed back into the main current. The tree-trunk bridge that lay across the creek was completely under water in three places. Laura began to struggle over it, half stumbling, half crawling in the darkening dusk. Her cap was torn off by an overhanging branch, and her thick brown hair hung down in wet strings and lay flat against her back. She knew if she made it about two-thirds of the way across the creek, she could wade to the shore through the reeds that clustered up against the opposite bank.

About halfway across, a rush of water washed her shoe away and wrapped the hem of her petticoat around the stub of a branch. She tore the petticoat loose and pushed forward. The water was getting deeper. She inched along the trunk, testing each hold. She knew that she must not falter now. As she drew nearer to the opposite bank, she reached the thick marsh reeds that swayed in a gentler current along the edge of the creek. She tightened her hold on the tree trunk and lowered one leg down into the water until she could feel the mud oozing over the sides of Elizabeth's shoe. Then she slipped off the trunk and started wading toward the bank, waist-deep in the swirling water. The remaining shoe refused to come out of the murky creek-bed. She was barefoot.

As she parted the last bunch of reeds, the total fatigue she'd been labouring under for the last two hours enveloped her like a dark cloud. She dropped heavily onto the grassy bank and fell into a half-sleep.

Crickets chirped gently in the quiet darkness, but they could not blot out the memory of the rough, vengeful voice: *Now's our chance to get rid of that green sliver and his Bloody Boys.*

She was jolted awake by a rustling sound. Before she knew what she was doing, she jumped to her feet and stared ahead. A familiar choking smell assailed her. It was a skunk. She squinted through the darkness—she could see it sauntering up the hill in front of her. A false alarm, but she knew that she put herself in danger if she rested in the open.

She struggled up the rough ground. It was painful without shoes, and she felt almost too weak to climb the steep hill ahead. She was thankful, though, that she knew the area well. She and her husband and small children had picnicked here many times.

If she could just reach the top of the hill, she would only have to cross a couple of low, flat fields and one more hill. From there, on that second rise of land, she knew she would be able to see the De Cew family house, where the lieutenant had set up his headquarters.

As she pushed her tired body uphill, waves of doubt began to wash over her—the lieutenant might not believe her message. Perhaps, as James had suggested, Chapin had only been bragging to his guerrillas. After all, the only evidence of the planned attack she had was the snippet of conversation she had overheard through the window. FitzGibbon might just laugh at her or pity her, thinking she had become confused from the pressures of the war or the heat of the day. She could just imagine him saying, "Madam, I'm truly sorry; I'll be needin' hard facts." Laura put these thoughts out of her mind and kept going up the hill.

The night was darker now. A thin wash of moonlight was all that lit the way. Without slowing her pace, she reached ahead to part the tall grass and weeds. She flinched as she stepped on a sharp stone, but the throbbing of her foot was lost in the pain she felt all over her body. She had been running, stumbling, walking for sixteen hours. It seemed that every muscle was screaming in pain. She did not even stop to check the new wound.

When she reached the top of the hill, she stopped abruptly,

trembling at an unexpected sight. Clusters of tents and groups of men around campfires were silhouetted against the sky.

At least a dozen men started to move toward her. As they came closer, she recognized the Mohawk leggings that some of them were wearing, but she could not guess the identity of the others. She wondered if they were on the side of the lieutenant. Whoever they were, they were now moving swiftly in her direction. As they come closer, she saw that they were staring at her with cold eyes and moving in to surround her. The two on the right pointed at her and began shouting to each other in a language she did not understand. She gasped in fear, but even as that terrible feeling of weakness came over her, she marched directly up to the one who appeared to be a chief and, pointing to the next hill, she said in a firm, sharp voice, "Lead me to Lieutenant FitzGibbon." She knew the lieutenant and his men were camped in the direction she was pointing. Surely he would understand.

But the chief just stood and looked at her. She motioned and pointed to the chief, then to herself, and then to the camp over the hill. She repeated these motions and said the lieutenant's name over and over. She kept the chief's attention. Then she pointed to the distant northeast and shouted, "The enemy is coming!"

The chief studied her closely, and finally his brow relaxed a little and his eyes became softer. He nodded, then turned and spoke to his men, but they looked suspiciously at her and spoke to each other in low voices.

Her heart pounded. She found it harder than ever to control her fear, but she was too tired to run away. All she could do was stand and wait.

The chief finally indicated that she should go with him. He and two of his men strode along beside her. She walked briskly with pain in every step, fearing that the chief would change his mind before they got there. Her breath came in short gasps, almost as if she were running again.

Laura had no idea how long it would take to reach the top of the last knoll. All she knew was that she could finally see the stone house where the lieutenant was stationed. As soon as it was in sight, one of the Mohawks ran ahead, but she could go no faster. She knew that she must not fall now, so near the end of her journey.

The darkness seemed to close in on her when she finally reached the yard in front of the house. The lieutenant, carrying a lantern, came out the front door and down the stone steps to meet them. She could not make out his features; her eyes were so blurred from fatigue.

She staggered as she reached him and gasped out her message. "I am the wife of Sergeant James Secord, who was wounded in active duty at the Battle of Queenston Heights."

Lieutenant FitzGibbon breathed in sharply and stared at

her in disbelief. Then he recovered himself and stared at her with his cool green eyes.

Laura tried to focus on the face before her. It looked familiar, somehow. "Since my husband is not able to travel, I have brought this message. The enemy under Colonel Boerstler and directed by Chapin's guerrillas plan a surprise attack tomorrow. They have a much larger force than you."

"Who told you this?"

She hesitated. Would the lieutenant take seriously the gossip of Chapin and his men? Could she tell him that the wine she served may well have loosened their tongues? "My husband does not wish to reveal his source, but he says to tell you it is a reliable one."

"How could you possibly have come by the road from St. David's? Enemy scouts are patrolling all the way to Queenston along the route."

"I know. I came 'round by the Great Black Swamp and Shipman's Corners. Then I went south and across Twelve Mile Creek to the Mohawks' camp."

The lieutenant's eyes narrowed with suspicion as he examined her wet, torn, blood-stained clothes, her scratched arms and legs, and her bleeding feet. "My God, Laura Ingersoll! If it's not Laura Ingersoll, I'll be—and you walked. My God, that's nineteen miles in this burning heat!"

How does he know my name? thought Laura, who was

trembling with fatigue. She looked up at him but could not make out the face exactly. It was a blur, and so were the other faces around him. Then, for a short moment, everything came into focus. It was Red. That was why he knew her name— Lieutenant James FitzGibbon was Red!

"Laura, I don't know how your husband got this information, but I believe you—you risked your life to get here."

Then, turning to one of his officers, he commanded, "Here, Sam, help this lady upstairs to Mrs. De Cew. She's about to faint. Move sharp now."

Red turned and walked briskly back to his headquarters. It was going to be a long night.

TWENTY-THREE

The first clank of cow bells sounded loudly in the morning air. Then four more rang out over the fields, one after the other, at even intervals.

"They've come," FitzGibbon announced to his men. It was seven a.m. on the twenty-fourth of June. FitzGibbon and his force of forty-five men had been waiting since late in the evening of the twenty-second when Laura had brought them her message.

Lieutenant FitzGibbon did one more quick calculation of the resources available to him. He had sent word to Major De Haren, who was camped a couple of miles to the north. At most, though, he reckoned that De Haren had no more than two hundred men. The opposing enemy force was made up of five hundred or more trained soldiers.

The lieutenant marshalled the Caughnawagas from Quebec, under Dominique Ducharme, the Grand River Mohawks led by the young John Brant, his second cousin, Captain William Johnson Kerr, and the tribe's adopted Scottish leader, John Norton. He instructed them to hide in the beech woods and to attack the fringes of the enemy from their secure position in the woods. The Indians numbered well over two hundred, and he knew he could depend on them to complete their task. They had proved their value and their loyalty many times in this war. His situation would be hopeless without them.

Still, FitzGibbon worried about how long they would last if face-to-face fighting followed. They were not accustomed to that kind of warfare. Still, the warriors who supported him were hidden and waiting.

At best, his circumstances were not good, even though he had received sufficient warning. If De Haren's troops arrived, he might have a chance. Without them, he would be far outnumbered by the attacking Americans. Yet he would not back down without a fight.

The enemy, unaware their every move was being watched by the Indians in the forest, moved steadily ahead. They had just completed a long march in the oppressive heat the day before. That night, as they slept in a nearby farmer's field, no light or fire was allowed, since that would reveal their position to the residents of Queenston. Extra scouts and guards had gone ahead of them as they marched out of the field, to make sure no one could possibly surprise the advancing troops.

Lieutenant FitzGibbon walked to a high spot on the top of a hill and looked over the cornfield. He could see the enemy. Soldiers in grey uniforms led the way. Next came the colonel on his horse, followed by what must be three hundred walking soldiers. Their dark blue shakos, blue coats, and white breeches would make them easily recognized targets. Behind the infantry came their train of artillery, with horse teams pulling wagons of ammunition and large and small field guns. More companies followed, each one led by its officer. In the rear were two dozen cavalrymen. The harnesses on their horses and brass plates on their caps flashed in the light of the morning sun.

Through his field glass, FitzGibbon saw the advance guard return after they had reconnoitred the woods. The main body of troops then proceeded to enter the beech woods. They were only a few miles now from his camp. When would the Mohawks and Caughnawagas attack the enemy? Watching the troops disappear into the woods, he drew in his breath and waited for the sounds of battle.

Suddenly, rifle shots and the piercing war cries of the warriors broke the silence of the morning. For a moment, relief swept over him.

FitzGibbon faced again the truth of his precarious position. What good were his forty-five soldiers and two hundred warriors against a trained enemy force of over five hundred regulars with more ammunition and supplies? Reinforcements could well come to them from Fort George before his own help arrived. If De Haren had really been only two miles away, he should have been here some time ago.

If the Americans emerged on the west side of the beech woods, only two short miles would lie between them and his men. Even with severe losses to the enemy, the Bloody Boys would be far outnumbered. He swallowed as he thought of his loyal crew, the men of the brave 49th Regiment with their scant numbers and meagre resources, fighting a well-supplied American army of five hundred. He could not let this happen.

When the enemy began to emerge from the far end of the woods, the Indians would lose ground. Only FitzGibbon's trained men could fight in the clearing, and those men would be swamped.

FitzGibbon's plan was too fantastic to dwell on for long. He moved speedily to the far end of the field and, when he reached his men, he had his bugler sound the cease fire. To his own surprise, the Indian attackers immediately fell silent in the woods and their firing stopped.

Holding high a white handkerchief firmly tied to his sword, he rode forward at a measured pace from the west toward the beech woods. FitzGibbon rode in silence, the white handkerchief fluttering weakly in the wind. There was not a single movement from the enemy side. He was getting dangerously close to their lines. He would be completely vulnerable.

Finally, an enemy soldier holding another white flag came toward him on a large white horse. The horse cantered at a controlled speed, then lightly pawed the ground when its master drew the reins in tightly to bring the steed to a stop.

"Good morning, sir," the officer said. "I am Roderick McDowell, First Regiment of Artillery, United States Army."

FitzGibbon put his bold plan into words. "My pleasure, sir. I am Lieutenant James FitzGibbon of His Majesty's Forty-ninth. I am instructed by Major De Haren to offer you the opportunity to surrender and avoid unnecessary bloodshed."

The officer did not reply.

"You are surrounded by a large force of British and cannot escape," FitzGibbon continued. "My Indian allies, incensed by their losses in this morning's battle, are ready to close in for a massacre. Only a fast surrender will ensure your safety."

"Thank you, Lieutenant. I shall relay Major De Haren's message to Colonel Boerstler," Captain McDowell replied. Nodding, he turned and then galloped back to his lines.

FitzGibbon waited patiently but his thoughts were racing ahead. He was planning the reply he would make if the colonel refused to surrender.

Just then, a British officer rode toward him from his own lines. "I'm Captain Hall from Chippawa. We heard firing, and I've come with my twenty dragoons. We're at your service, Lieutenant."

"Thank you, Captain Hall. Please return to your lines, but I may call you back shortly. In the absence of Major De Haren, you may have to impersonate him."

Captain Hall looked puzzled. "Only in the eyes of the enemy," FitzGibbon told him and laughed loudly. Quite puzzled, Captain Hall nodded and returned to his men.

In a short time, Captain McDowell returned with his commander's message. "Colonel Boerstler says he is not in the habit of surrendering to an army he has never seen."

With an expression of confidence, FitzGibbon replied, "If that is his wish, I shall ask my superior officer if I may escort Colonel Boerstler to see our troops."

FitzGibbon abruptly pulled his horse's right rein, and the animal turned so suddenly its raised tail cut the air in a semi-circle. He galloped back to his men, went directly to Hall, and saluted him.

The amazed officer still did not realize what was happening. In a low voice, he stammered, "Lieutenant, I don't understand."

"Captain, you don't need to. But, for the present just pretend you are my superior officer. I want the enemy to believe that you are Major De Haren. If all goes well, you will be no closer to the enemy than you are now. Later, it won't matter if they discover that you aren't Major De Haren." As he spoke, FitzGibbon gestured with his hands and pointed to the enemy.

He shook his head several times and pointed again.

Hall was becoming more confused. "It's all for effect," FitzGibbon said. "They may be watching."

Finally, he nodded his head and saluted Hall. Still holding his horse's reins, he mounted lightly and cantered back to the enemy.

FitzGibbon watched as Colonel Boerstler advanced slowly toward him. Even though his horse was moving at an even speed, the officer grimaced with each shift in position. Fitz-Gibbon looked at the grave-faced colonel and sized him up. He was not a big man, and he had a sallow, pale complexion. Then he looked down and saw that blood had hardened on the colonel's uniform just above his saddle and down his leg. The colonel sat with great discomfort on his horse.

FitzGibbon saluted the colonel. "I am sorry, sir," FitzGibbon said, "but Major De Haren refuses to put his troops on display for the enemy."

Weakened from his loss of blood, Boerstler hesitated. "We need time to decide. Ask Major De Haren to give us until sundown."

"Sundown!" shouted the agitated FitzGibbon. "No, Colonel Boerstler, we cannot give you the time you request. I can't promise you any more than five minutes. My Indian allies are chafing to avenge the death of their friends."

FitzGibbon forced himself to speak more slowly. "I am

aware that the Americans accuse us of stimulating the Indians to destroy you, whereas we have ever used our best endeavour, and almost always successfully, to protect you."

In extreme pain, Colonel Boerstler replied, "Can you, in fact, ensure the safety of my men?"

Heartened by his reply but reluctant to show it, FitzGibbon avowed, "I can only give you this assurance—the Indians must take my life before they shall attack you."

"Your assurance is sufficient!" Boerstler explained and held out his hand to FitzGibbon.

With great reserve and considerable gravity, FitzGibbon took the officer's hand. He dared not look too jubilant.

Then, as he started to discuss the details for surrender, he noticed a horse galloping speedily toward him. To his amazement, the real Major De Haren was rapidly approaching, accompanied by his aide.

FitzGibbon turned and rode back to meet him. After he had saluted, he quickly asked, "Do you have your troops?"

"No, Lieutenant," the major replied. "They're miles away, but I'm here. I'll take over now."

"Sir, I already have control. They have surr—"

As Major De Haren brushed by FitzGibbon to face the enemy, with no knowledge of the negotiations underway, FitzGibbon groaned. Would all be lost now?

Inflamed, he turned and raced his horse to De Haren's side

and said in a low, bold tone, so only the major could hear, "Not another word, sir, not another word. These men are my prisoners."

Before the major had time to reply, FitzGibbon addressed him loudly so that the enemy could hear. "Shall I proceed to disarm the American troops?"

De Haren answered, "You have my permission."

As the American troops lined up before them, FitzGibbon watched De Haren, who was now beside Boerstler. Would De Haren say something that might give away the ruse? Then, in a flash, he thought of a solution.

He barked a command to the soldiers. "American troops, right face. Quick march." Boerstler nodded to his officers, and they repeated the command to the men. As the troops marched straight ahead, the two leaders had to move apart and were prevented from talking to each other.

The Americans were approaching the wooded area where FitzGibbon's men were waiting, so the lieutenant addressed De Haren, "Sir, shall the American troops ground their arms here?"

"No," he answered harshly. "Let them march through between our men and ground their arms on the other side."

FitzGibbon seethed inwardly. In his desire to humiliate the enemy by forcing them to lay down their arms before their conquerors, De Haren had forgotten one important fact. Would five hundred men lay down their arms when they saw they were facing a force of only forty-five? He thought not.

Lieutenant FitzGibbon drew a deep breath. "Sir, do you think it prudent to march them through with arms in their hands in the presence of the Indians?" he shouted to De Haren.

"For God's sake, sir, do what this officer bids you!" Colonel Boerstler shouted to De Haren.

"Do so," De Haren told him.

"Americans, halt! Front! Ground your arms!" FitzGibbon shouted. The command was passed on by the American officers.

They obeyed promptly. The Indians rushed out of the woods and headed straight for the soldiers. They had been promised the enemy's weapons in return for doing them no harm. A few American soldiers, terrorized as they watched the Indians approach, reached down for their muskets.

Instantly, FitzGibbon's voice rang out, "Americans, don't touch your arms! Not a hair of your head shall be hurt. Remember, I am here."

Lieutenant FitzGibbon started to relax now. He knew he could rely on the word of the chiefs.

He turned to Colonel Boerstler. "Come with me," he commanded in a kind, courteous tone. "I will take you to my headquarters at the De Cew house where you will receive care for your wounds."

TWENTY-FOUR

Laura awakened from her sleep to the sound of rifles. At first, startled by the realization that she was in strange surroundings, she swung her feet abruptly to the floor. Pain shot to her head. Gingerly, she started toward the door. Then she remembered where she was and sat down on the side of the bed.

She did recall reaching Lieutenant FitzGibbon with her message about the surprise attack. She also remembered that Mrs. De Cew had taken her upstairs to wash her bleeding feet and give her soft shoes. A waiting officer then had escorted her to this farmhouse—a few fields away. Inside, she had vaguely recognized Mrs. Turney, who had helped her upstairs to this comfortable bed.

I must have slept right off, she thought as she looked around the small, clean room. She remembered nothing about the room from the night before. Just past the two oak posts at the foot of her bed, the pale blue chintz curtains blew gently in the breeze. Nearer the door, there was a small washstand with a jug and bowl, clean towels, and a dish of soft soap.

The gunfire started again as Laura headed for the door. She winced. Her feet were wrapped in strips of a white linen shift.

"Hello," Laura called out at the top of the stairs.

She heard light steps below. A woman hurried up the straight, steep stairs toward her.

"Mrs. Secord, how are you?" she asked before she reached the top of the stairs.

"I'm quite well," Laura replied, "... although a little light-headed, I'm afraid."

"Just you go right back to bed," the woman said as she took her hand. "I'm Mary Turney. A soldier and my husband brought you here the night before last. You were worn right out."

Laura did not know the Turneys personally, but she recognized the woman's face and knew the farmhouse where she had slept. "The night before last—you mean, I've slept since then?"

"Yes, you have."

"And the fighting? Has it been going on all this time?"

"Oh, no. The fighting just got started. Lieutenant Fitz-Gibbon sent men out to watch. They watched through all that night and yesterday and last night."

"So, now they've come."

"I don't rightly know, but they must have, for there's

shooting now. I'm sure it's not a turkey shoot that's going on. Though I've not heard any cannons."

"Did British soldiers arrive in time to help?"

"Don't you worry yourself. Lieutenant FitzGibbon is taking care of it. His men have been planning for it ever since you came. You just sit right on your bed until I get back up here with some soup. That light head will be gone in no time."

Laura lay on the bed and thought of her meeting with FitzGibbon. At the time, she was sure he was really Red, but now she was beginning to doubt it. After all, she had been in a state of extreme exhaustion and could easily have been confused. But whether FitzGibbon was really Red or not, the important thing was that she had delivered her message, and FitzGibbon, whoever he was, had acted on it.

Before long, Mrs. Turney came back with a bowl of soup and a cup of steaming coffee. She hurried back downstairs to her baby. As Laura sipped the hot coffee, her thoughts went back to Queenston.

She wondered how her family had fared as the American army marched through. Had her daughters and Fan and Bob been able to carry on in her absence? If she were missed by the scouts, would the authorities accept the explanation that she was visiting her brother in St. David's? Then, as she took sips of the soup, she realized that the American soldiers would be too busy planning an attack to look for a missing wife and mother. Her family were fine, no doubt. The danger was possibly nearer at hand.

"You finished that soup yet?" Mrs. Turney called up to Laura.

"Yes, thank you."

"Can I bring you some more?"

"No, thank you."

Mrs. Turney climbed the steep stairs and puffed a little as she put down a pair of leather slippers for Laura. "You may need these when you feel like getting up. Here, let me help you with the bandages." She moved toward Laura.

"No, thank you. I can do this myself."

"Well, if you're sure you can manage. I should get back down to my kitchen work. But just you call if there's anything else you need." Mrs. Turney turned and left the room and walked heavily down the stairs.

Laura slowly unwrapped her bandaged feet. They were still swollen, but not too painful now, and she was able to fit them into the slippers. For a minute, she lay back on the bed and tried to sleep. But she was too restless. She needed to be doing something to take her mind off her family—and the battle a few fields away. It was strangely quiet for a battle so near. Whatever had happened? She felt her way down the narrow back stairs and then went on out to the kitchen.

"I'd like to help," she told Mrs. Turney, who was peeling potatoes at the sink.

"Now, that's not necessary. You just go back to bed."

"No, I'd really rather work. It'll pass the time."

* * *

Laura and Mrs. Turney sat silently in the kitchen, wondering what was happening. Had the battle ended so quickly, and who had won? They listened for the whoops of victorious Indians. If they heard these, they would know that the victory had gone to Upper Canada.

Finally, Mrs. Turney said, "We'd best be preparing some supper." She bustled over to the pantry and came out with the leftover potatoes in the iron spider frying pan, which she set on the back table. "Here, you slice these, dear." She handed Laura a knife and went back to her pantry for more victuals.

Laura's hands trembled a little as she sliced the potatoes. She strained to hear the sounds that did not come. She started chopping the sliced potatoes.

"We don't need those potatoes for mincemeat," Mrs. Turney said, then added more gently, "Thank you, dear. They'll do just fine."

Laura nodded as she looked down at the potatoes, all chopped into little bits.

It was nearly five when they heard the sound of someone running toward the house. Mrs. Turney swung the door open and her husband burst in.

"They've surrendered. It's all over. And the lieutenant wants to see Mrs. Secord before I take her home." It was then they heard the jubilant whoops of the victorious Mohawks and Caughnawagas.

* * *

The following afternoon, Red sat alone at his desk in the De Cew house when Laura entered. She had not been dreaming. It really was Red.

When the door closed behind her, FitzGibbon reached out for Laura's hand and clasped it in both of his. "They surrendered without a battle," he declared. "And it's all because of you that we were ready for them. We would have lost without your warning. How can I thank you?"

She gave him a mischievous smile and said, "I always seem to be getting you out of tight spots, don't I?"

He laughed that merry boyish laugh that she remembered from so many years ago and motioned her to a chair by his desk. He pulled his own chair out from behind his desk and sat close beside her.

She drew her swollen feet in under her chair. When she looked up, he was still staring at her. He seemed to be speechless.

"So, FitzGibbon is your real name?" she asked, still nagged by lingering doubts.

"Yes, it's James FitzGibbon, but I couldn't tell you that when I visited your home—for I was going on a fishing expedition into the enemy camp to discover their strengths and resources."

"I understand that," she said, "but I do not understand the rest. What are you doing in Canada, and how did you find your way into the British army?"

"Well, after I sailed back to Ireland, I ended up back home on Bantry Bay. I worked hard on my father's small farm and occasionally caught a salmon to help feed the family. Then, when I was fifteen, a French fleet invaded our area, and troops were sent in from England to protect us. The first regiment to appear in our village were the Devon and Cornwall Fencibles, who were billeted in our homes. Their quiet behaviour and gratitude for our hospitality astounded me, for the whole village had little use for the English."

"So, you ran away and joined the army when you were old enough?"

"Not exactly. I had neither the money nor the education to become a commissioned officer and so was reluctant at first to join up."

"So, how did it happen?"

"Friends and a lot of luck." A sad expression crept across his face, and Laura did not question him further, for she had heard that FitzGibbon was a protégé of the great Sir Isaac Brock.

"Well, it is our good fortune that you were here to save us from the enemy. All Upper Canada would have been lost without you." She spoke more formally now, but as she stood up, she added, "And, Red, you know I've never forgotten you over the years. There were many times when I missed you and wondered what had become of you."

Red smiled a proud lieutenant's smile, but there was something impish in it. "Now, don't say you were pining. You've had plenty to keep you occupied with a husband and children."

"Of course, but you still had a special place in my heart. Don't slip out of sight again, Red. Come and see me and my family as soon as you can."

"I will, Laura." He rose from his chair.

Laura smiled at her old friend and stood to leave. Then a look of fear crept into her eyes. "I have just one request, Red."

"What is it?"

"Please don't tell anyone that I brought you this message. We are not safe from the enemy. Today, you have won the battle, but tomorrow, who knows who will rule the Peninsula?"

"Don't concern yourself, Laura," said FitzGibbon, his eyes twinkling. "Nothing will be said, but I feel confident we will drive the Americans back home."

"I hope you are right, Red. God be with you in our defence."

* * *

Mr. Turney's vegetable wagon crept along at a snail's pace toward Queenston. Laura sat up on the buckboard beside the farmer, trying not to shout at him to hurry along. She had been gone for only four days, but she was getting more anxious about her family the closer they got to the village.

"I'll just keep moving slow and easy up to your house, Mrs. Secord," Mr. Turney said, peering through the gathering dusk. "No point in arousing suspicion. We have the Americans on the run now, but who knows what next month will bring?"

Laura nodded but was still impatient. This trip back to Queenston seemed to be taking longer than the trek to Beaver Dams. Finally, as they reached the edge of the village, they turned out from the woods that lined the roadway and started down her street. She could hear the creak of the well-crank turning in the backyard, but, apart from that, all was silent. The red roses overhanging the front walk blossomed quietly; it was as if nothing had happened.

Mr. Turney pulled the reins tightly and his horses stopped in front of the house. "Everything seems to be fine," he said, "but I'll wait here in case you need help. If all is well, you can wave me on. I have business to attend to at the Landing."

Laura jumped down lightly from the side of the wagon as he finished speaking. She winced a little as her feet touched the ground. "Thank you," she said. "Thank you for everything."

Ignoring the pain from her bruised feet, Laura ran up the path toward the front door. The smell of roses gathered in around her like a bride's veil. She walked up the stone steps and threw open the door. Inside, the hall was quiet and dark. All she could hear was the clock ticking in the parlour. The kitchen was empty, but the table had been set for the next morning's breakfast. Laura ran back to the front door and waved Mr. Turney on.

"I'm home, James, I'm home," she shouted as she ran back down the hall toward the stairs. She raised the muddied hem of her borrowed petticoat and ran up the steps. James had still not answered her. The upper hallway was as silent as the downstairs. But when she looked up toward the bedroom, she saw him. He was standing, but he was so weak that he had to lean against the doorway.

She ran to him and threw her arms gently around him.

"Thank God! Thank God!" James whispered, clasping her to him.

For a minute they stood there, silently holding each other.

Then he asked, "Laura, did you reach FitzGibbon?"

"Yes, and the American soldiers have surrendered. The British have control of the Peninsula again."

"Do the Americans know how their surprise was found out?"

"I asked FitzGibbon not to reveal my part, in case there were more American attacks. He will keep my secret. We are safe, James. We are safe."

James limped back to his chair and sank into it, grimacing with pain. In the dying light of the sun, Laura could see deep lines around his mouth that she had not noticed before. She sat on the footstool beside his chair and reached across to take his hand. It was warm and strong. It gave her hope that his health would soon be completely restored.

They sat together at the end of the day and looked out the window toward Queenston Heights.

THE ROUTE OF LAURA'S WALK

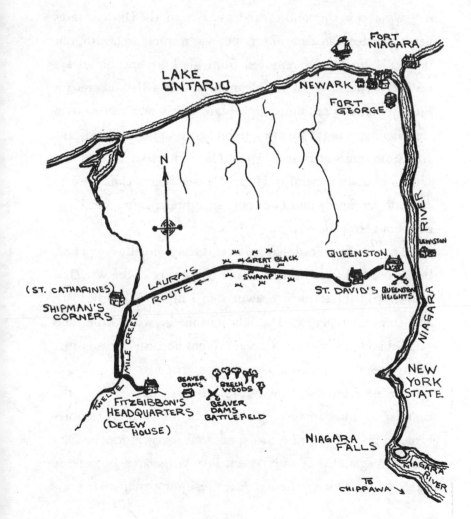

HISTORICAL NOTE

The war with the Americans ended eighteen months after Laura's walk, and peace came to Queenston. No Canadian territory was lost in the conflict, and, as a nation, the United States never invaded Canada again. James was restored to health, but the bullet never was removed from his knee and he always walked with a limp. At Kingston in January 1814, Lieutenant FitzGibbon was promoted to captain of his own company of the Glengarry Light Infantry, in recognition for capturing the American forces at Beaver Dams. He later rose to colonel and acting adjutant general in Upper Canada. Laura continued to care for her family and two more daughters, Laura and Hannah, born after the war.

The major events described in this story actually happened, but Laura had five children at the beginning of the war. The character of Elizabeth is drawn from Laura's sister Elizabeth and step-sister Nancy. The relationship between Laura and FitzGibbon is fictitious. Captain Wool and the Secords met again after the war and became lifelong friends.

James's business in Queenston did not recover from the plundering and damage of the war, but his business troubles came to an end when he was appointed registrar for the District Surrogate Court of Niagara. Five years later, he became judge of the District Court. After resigning from that position in 1835, he became collector of customs in Chippawa. The income from that job and his small military pension were enough to keep his family living comfortably.

In 1841, less than a decade after he took the customs job, James died. He was sixty-seven and Laura was sixty-five at the time. He was buried in Drummond Hill Cemetery in Niagara Falls, the site of the battle of Lundy's Lane, the last and the bloodiest fight of the war of 1812–14, where many of his fellow soldiers had fallen.

Laura never received official recognition during her lifetime from the British colonial government or the Canadian government for her part in the victory at Beaver Dams, and, in later years, historians questioned whether Laura had actually brought FitzGibbon any information he did not already have. Laura's descendants were quite sure that FitzGibbon's victory was the result of Laura's message, and they would not give up searching for proof. Through the efforts of one of these descendants, Henry Cartwright Secord, a certificate written by FitzGibbon in 1820, testifying to the fact that Laura Secord had brought him a message of an impending attack at Beaver Dams, was located in 1934. Its contents were similar to those of an existing certificate that FitzGibbon had written in 1837, but its date, closer to the time of the event, made it more valid.

Then, in 1959, the third and most important certificate was found in the National Archives at Ottawa. In it, FitzGibbon gave the exact date of Laura Secord's walk and drew attention to the fact that her message reached him first. He pointed out that "Mrs. Secord and her Family were entire Strangers to [him] before the 22nd of June 1813, and her exertions therefore could have been made from public motives only." But it was the following statement that provided the best proof that FitzGibbon was unaware of the planned attack by Chapin and his guerrillas: "In consequence of this information," he wrote, "I placed Indians under Norton together with my Detachment in a Situation to intercept the American Detachment." After this discovery, Laura Secord's heroic act and its direct benefit to FitzGibbon were recognized and described in textbooks.

Laura did receive recognition for her heroism from the British government when she was in her eighties. In 1860, Albert Edward, Prince of Wales, then a young man of nineteen, was visiting Niagara. He had been asked to officiate at a Queenston Heights ceremony in which Laura's name appeared on the list of war veterans presented to the Prince. He became interested in Laura's story, as she was the only woman among the veterans. In 1861, after he returned home, he sent her 100 pounds in gold in appreciation for her service to her country. Prince Albert Edward later became King Edward VII.

Laura Secord died on October 17, 1868, twenty-seven years after her husband's death. She was ninety-three years old. In 1901, a monument was erected above her grave in Drummond

Hill Cemetery, where she is buried beside James. Beneath a sculptured bust of this courageous woman is the following inscription:

TO PERPETUATE
THE NAME AND FAME OF
LAURA SECORD
WHO WALKED ALONE NEARLY 20
MILES BY CIRCUITOUS, DIFFICULT
AND PERILOUS ROUTE THROUGH WOODS
AND SWAMPS AND OVER MIRY ROADS
TO WARN A BRITISH OUTPOST AT
DE CEW'S FALLS OF AN INTENDED ATTACK
AND THEREBY ENABLED LIEUT. FITZGIBBON
ON THE 24TH JUNE, 1813, WITH LESS
THAN 50 MEN OF H.M. 49TH REGT.
ABOUT 15 MILITIA MEN AND A SMALL
FORCE OF SIX NATION AND OTHER INDIANS
UNDER CAPTAIN WILLIAM JOHNSON KERR
AND DOMINIQUE DUCHARME, TO SURPRISE
AND ATTACK THE ENEMY AT BEECHWOODS
(OR BEAVER DAMS), AND AFTER A SHORT
ENGAGEMENT TO CAPTURE COL. BOERSTLER
OF THE U.S. ARMY AND HIS ENTIRE FORCE
OF 542 MEN WITH TWO FIELD PIECES.

The Government of Canada erected a second monument to Laura Secord in 1910. This monument stands twelve feet high, not far from Brock's gigantic monument on Queenston Heights. This is its inscription:

TO LAURA INGERSOLL SECORD
WHO SAVED HER HUSBAND'S LIFE
IN THE BATTLE OF THESE HEIGHTS
OCTOBER 13TH, 1812
AND WHO RISKED HER OWN
IN CONVEYING TO CAPT. FITZGIBBON
INFORMATION BY WHICH HE WON
THE VICTORY OF BEAVER DAMS.

This second monument is not far from the place where Laura found and rescued her husband during the Battle of Queenston Heights. Many have come to read the inscriptions and to look out over the Niagara River as James and Laura did two centuries ago.

NOTES

The following are explanatory notes and sources for quotations and references. The numbers along the left refer to the page numbers in *Acts of Courage: Laura Secord and The War of 1812.*

19   "Better... than the halter." (These words were the slogan of the men in Shay's rebellion.) Judge Whiting in the records of the Massachusetts Supreme Judicial Court in the Suffock County Courthouse in Boston under #160304 in Marion L. Starkey, *A Little Rebellion* (New York: Alfred A. Knopf Inc., 1955), p. 174.

148   "As sure as you do, I will have you indicted for murder." Laura Secord as related by her granddaughter, Mrs. Cockburn, in Emma A. Currie, *The Story of Laura Secord and Canadian Reminiscences* (Toronto: William Briggs, 1900), p. 69.

196   "When we come for good to this country, we'll divide the land, and I'll take this here for my share." American soldier as told to Mrs. Curzon in *The Story of Laura Secord*, p. 66.

196   "You scoundrel, all you'll ever get here will be six feet of earth." Laura Secord in *The Story of Laura Secord*, p. 66.

199 "You were right about the six feet of earth, missus," American soldier in *The Story of Laura Secord*, p. 66.

215 "James, somebody ought to tell Lieutenant FitzGibbon they are coming." Laura Secord as related by Laura Secord Clark, granddaughter of Laura Secord, to Mrs. George S. Henry, Ontario Dept. of Public Records and Archives, Misc., 1933 and Ruth McKenzie, *Laura Secord, The Legend and the Lady* (Toronto: McClelland & Stewart, 1971), p. 51.

215 "Well, if I crawled on my hands and knees, I could not get there in time." James Secord in *Laura Secord*, p. 51.

215 "Well, suppose I go?" Laura Secord in *Laura Secord*, p. 51.

215 "You go? With the country in so disturbed a state? I doubt a man could get through, let alone a woman." James Secord in *Laura Secord*, p. 51.

215 "You forget, James, that God will take care of me." Laura Secord in *Laura Secord*, p.51.

238–239 "I am aware...to protect you." FitzGibbon in Mary Agnes FitzGibbon, *A Veteran of 1812: The Life of James FitzGibbon* (Toronto: William Briggs, 1894), p. 88.

239 "I can only give...shall attack you." FitzGibbon in *A Veteran of 1812*, p.89.

240 "Not another word…are my prisoners." FitzGibbon in *A Veteran of 1812*, p. 90.

240 "American troops, right face. Quick march." FitzGibbon in *A Veteran of 1812*, p. 90.

240 "…shall the American troops ground their arms here?" FitzGibbon in *A Veteran of 1812*, p. 90.

240 "Let… on the other side." Major De Haren in *A Veteran of 1812*, p. 91.

241 "…do you think it prudent… of the Indians?" FitzGibbon in *A Veteran of 1812*, p. 91.

241 "For God's sake, sir, do what this officer bids you!" Boerstler in *A Veteran of 1812*, p. 91.

241 "Do so." De Haren in *A Veteran of 1812*, p. 91.

241 "Americans, halt! … Ground your arms!" FitzGibbon in *A Veteran of 1812*, p. 91.

241 "Americans, don't touch your arms! … Remember, I am here." FitzGibbon in *A Veteran of 1812*, p. 91.

242 "…slept right off." Laura Secord in *A Veteran of 1812*, p. 85.

OTHER BOOKS BY CONNIE BRUMMEL CROOK

NOVELS

The Meyers Saga
Flight
Meyers' Creek
Meyers' Rebellion
The Nellie McClung trilogy
Nellie L.
Nellie's Quest
Nellie's Victory
Historical Years in Upper Canada: Ontario
The Hungry Year
The Perilous Year
No Small Victory

PICTURE BOOKS

Maple Moon (Lune d'érable)
Laura Secord's Brave Walk

CHAPTER BOOK
Mary's Way

Connie Brummel Crook is an historian, former teacher, and the author of more than a dozen historical books for children that often focus on the history of Upper Canada. One of her books on the 1837 Rebellion in Upper Canada, *Meyers' Rebellion*, was a Geoffrey Bilson Fiction Award finalist. Her picture book, *Maple Moon*, was a Storytelling World Honour Title winner. Connie lives in Peterborough, Ontario.